I0691407

Clydesdale

GOES TO WASHINGTON

First Edition

Published by The Nazca Plains Corporation
Las Vegas, Nevada
2010

ISBN: 978-1-935509-91-2

Published by

The Nazca Plains Corporation ®
4640 Paradise Rd, Suite 141
Las Vegas NV 89109-8000

PUBLISHER'S NOTE
Clydesdale Goes to Washington is a work of fiction created wholly
by *Bob Archman*'s imagination. All characters are fictional and any
resemblance to any persons living or deceased is purely by accident.
No portion of this book reflects any real person or events.

Cover Photos,
Christopher Howey and Mazuciukas

Art Director,
Blake Stephens

Clydesdale

GOES TO WASHINGTON

First Edition

Bob Archman

Part I

I was surprised when Edmund Willamette came by to see me. He was a board member of the local university and I had done some work for some friends of his. He was the president of a large insurance company. We had met once, but I only knew him casually.

"Mr. Noland," he said. "I spoke with one of my friends and he told me you could be trusted. I have a peculiar situation I don't know how to handle. I am a rather conventional man, and my experiences are limited. Please don't take offense at anything I say. A friend said you were gay and well acquainted with the gay community."

"Is that a problem?" I asked.

"Oddly, that is what I need," Willamette replied. "It's a problem with my older son. I realize he's gay, but there is something going on with him that worries me. He's in the Navy."

"Is this a don't ask, don't tell problem?"

"I don't think so, but I'm not sure," Willamette said. "He has been dipping into his trust fund heavily for the last few months. He's not buying a house and doesn't seem to have any unusual expenditures. I think he's being blackmailed."

"Have you asked him?"

"I tried and it wasn't a success," he said. "I did find out the monies were going to something called the Mandrake Club. It seems to be some sort of a men's social club in D.C."

"I'm afraid I don't much run in social club circles," I said. We talked for a while and I suggested he try to talk to his son again. "It may be something simple and innocent. I'd try talking again. Is he out?"

"Not at all," Willamette said. "He's moving up in the Navy and that would be disastrous for his career."

"Does he know you know?"

"No."

"Well, maybe you could let him know you support him regardless," I said. "He may be afraid of your reaction." Willamette agreed and left. I thought nothing more about the conversation until I saw a news story in the paper a few weeks later.

The headline read, "Body Found Floating in Tidal Basin." The article identified the body as Commander William D. Willamette. Cause of death unknown." The article went on to describe his career and background in Richmond. It was light on actual details of the death. I was unhappy about this; I was afraid it might be a suicide.

The funeral notice a day later referred to his death "under suspicious circumstances." That means murder. If it had been suicide, they normally wouldn't mention the cause of death at all.

The day after the funeral, Mr. Willamette came to my office again. He had talked with his son and his son had told him he was gay. "It was a great relief to him," Willamette said. "He said he had made some bad choices, but he would work it out. I asked if I could help, but he said I already had. Someone killed him a week later."

"Any clues?" I asked. "How are the police doing?"

"They aren't doing much," the distraught father said. "I talked with one of his friends, Lt. Commander Frederick, and asked if the Mandrake Club might have something to do with it. He turned white and said "Oh shit." He wouldn't tell me anymore."

"That sure sounds like a clue to me," I said. "Have you told the police?"

"No, not yet," he replied, "After Frederick's response I thought it might be good to do more investigating. I don't know the lie of the land. Can you help me?"

"I'll make some calls and see what's up," I said. He left. I called a few of my friends in D.C. The first two guys had never heard of the Mandrake Club, but one had a friend who was a congressional aide. He gave me the aide's number.

I called him that evening. It took a while to get him to talk. I gave him the names of some of my Richmond contacts and then he hung up. He called my friends and confirmed I was who I said I was, then called back.

"Is this Clydesdale?" he asked. When I said I was, he went on. "This is Roger, the guy you talked to earlier. You want to know about the Mandrake Club?"

"That's my interest," I said.

"How did you find out about it?" he asked. I told him about the Commander's death and Mr. Willamette's concerns. That satisfied Roger.

"Well, I really don't know much, but I have heard rumors," he said. I was sure he knew a lot more than rumors. He was in politics. "Technically it's a men's club, sort of like the type you found in Victorian England. The members are all distinguished upper crust gentlemen. Most aren't effeminate, but there is an air about the place."

"Do they all wear bow-ties and well-pressed shirts?" I asked.

"You got it. It has a distinctly conservative clientele," Roger said. "Some are Republicans, but others are to the right of that. Some are well to the right."

"Heil Hitler style?"

"Let's just say they like the great leader and captains of industry," Roger said. "Not my kind of men. I did run into one of the boys who works there. He's not my type either, but cute and very boyish."

"Virginal?"

Roger laughed. "He sure looked the part, but as Mae West said, "I use to be snow white, but I drifted." This kid had drifted from the Arctic wastes to the equator. He looks a good ten years younger than his age. He's thirty-years-old, but easily could pass for being a nineteen or twenty-year old. I would bet he could play a virgin well."

"Did he provide special services to the club members?" I asked.

Roger laughed again. "I don't know, but I would be surprised if he didn't. He likes older men and he wasn't the shy type. His interest in me dimmed when he discovered I wasn't a sugar Daddy." We talked for a while, and I decided to go to Washington and I asked if I could visit with him.

"Your friends told me you are a small guy," Roger said, "except where it counts."

"Are you a size queen?" I asked.

"No, but I do have an interest," Roger replied. "You could say I am a bit curious."

"I don't mind satisfying a guy's curiosity," I said. We agreed to meet on Thursday. After the call, I contacted Mr. Willamette and told him I had a modest lead.

"You know there's no way to know where an investigation might lead." I said. He told me he wanted to know what happened whatever that might be, "Something smells in Denmark."

I met Roger for dinner in a small, out of the way Georgetown restaurant. The place barely had a sign, but the food was good and the atmosphere was quiet and pleasant. At first, I thought Roger was forty, but as we chatted, I realized he was much closer to 60. He worked at looking young. He had been in Washington for a long while and knew the ropes.

The Mandrake Club was just barely in his radar range. He worked for liberal North Eastern representative, and was definitely not one of the elect who joined the Mandrake. "I'm not sure there's enough oxygen in the place to permit intelligent thought," he said. "Died in the wool reactionaries aren't my type. Most seem to be of the pompous and sanctimonious bent."

After dinner, we went to his apartment and Roger became a lot more talkative. We had a few drinks. I was taking a leak when he came in and checked me out. He liked my cock, but he really loved the piss. That isn't my thing, but I don't mind helping a guy out. Piss is piss as far as I can tell, but Roger had a spectacular orgasm as he drank mine. Afterwards, he apologetically told me he wasn't into anal much. He had checked me out with my friends in Richmond and knew my interests. I said it was okay.

We had another drink and he told me more about the Mandrake Club. He suspected there was a sexual aspect to it. His young playmate had mentioned the Club had lost its only horse-hung top and the members were unhappy about that. The young man had been otherwise discrete and that was his only slip.

"From the way he talked about the horse hung top, I think it wasn't only the members who missed him," Roger said. "There was some longing in his voice."

"I'd like to talk with this guy," I said.

"You're not his type, except for your cock. I do have his number; do you want me to call him?" Roger asked. "We'd have a lot better chance of getting him here it there was some show and tell."

"I'm willing, but maybe you can introduce me as your cousin, Clydesdale Noland, from out of town," I suggested. "I don't want anyone to know I'm here on business." Roger understood and called his friend, Lonnie.

Somehow, I became Roger's distant and very country cousin. "The guy looks like a straggly monkey, but he's hung like a fucking horse," I overheard Roger saying. "You've got to see it to believe it." Lonnie appeared at the apartment door a half hour later.

It wasn't love at first sight, but as soon as Lonnie saw my cock, all was well. I had stacked the deck by wearing a towel when we met. Once it dropped, my cock was the bait and Lonnie went for it. Roger was amused. Lonnie was a classic size queen. When he saw my cock, he had that deer caught in the headlights look to him. Lonnie just stared at it. Lonnie wasn't handsome. He was pretty. As Roger has said, he looked a lot younger than he was, but he worked at looking like a teenager.

Lonnie wasn't my type at all. He had that annoying tendency to treat you as if you were just there on approval. That is unattractive in successful men, but ugly in a waiter-gigolo. He was self confident, self-assured and he wouldn't have given me a second look if Roger hadn't clued him in on my cock.

Poor Lonnie was torn between desire for my cock and no attraction for me otherwise. I guessed my cock would win, and I was right. I also had a strong premonition once my cock was in his ass to the hilt, Lonnie would lose his airs.

After introductions, Roger said he was tired and was going to bed, but we could use the guest room if we wanted. The second Roger closed his bedroom door. Lonnie got naked. He was thin and hairless, except for his pubic bush. It took an entire three seconds to realize he wanted it in the ass.

Roger had cunningly left a tube of lubricant on the bedside table. Lonnie was small, but experienced. I fingered his ass and found he had already lubricated his hole. He twitched and shivered as I played with his ass. He wanted my cock badly, but he was tight. It almost took a shoehorn to get my cock in his ass. It took some work, but it was worth it.

Lonnie complained I was trying to split him in half at first, but the complaints turned into whimpers and then moans. I'm not opposed to combining work and pleasure. Lonnie wasn't my type, but he had a good ass and was a responsive bottom. Lonnie converted from being a stuck up twerp, to a genuinely appreciative bottom slut. From time to time, I caught him doing his whore routine. He cried, "I've never felt anything so big before," and "I've always liked older men." When he did this, I gave him a nice hard thrust and winded him.

After about five minutes of fucking, we got into the swing of things. He was one of those men who almost have a prehensile ass. He would open up his ass lips to let me in, then would try to clamp tight once I was in. I was having a good old time pumping hard when he exploded. There was cum everywhere. He must have lost a pound of two of his body weight. His love tunnel contacted and squeezed my cock every time he ejaculated. I've only known a few men who did that, and I shot my load deep in his love chute.

Much to my surprise, my climax set him off again. His second orgasm wasn't as spectacular as the first, but it was damn good.

"You're good at that," he said after he got his breath back. "I been worked over by one, or two guys and you're the best."

"I take it you aren't a virgin?" I asked.

"Well, to tell you the truth, if I have to be a virgin, it costs a little extra," he said. "I'm a waiter at a swank private club. For extra services I get more than a good tip, if you get my drift."

"If I could make a living fucking, I'd be a happy guy," I said. "It would sure beat working in a Seven-Eleven."

"Is that what you do?"

"I am between engagements," I said. "I'm here looking for a job. It has to be a lot easier to get a job here than in south-west Virginia. I've been a janitor, a prison guard and a locker room attendant as well as a cash register jockey."

"You like sex a lot?"

"Couldn't you tell?" I asked. "Some people might say I like sex way too much. I'm not young anymore, but it's still exciting to get into a new ass. My problem is I just like sex. I'm not much into romance. The modern style for gay men is to be all lovey-dovey. That ain't my style."

"You're not looking for a LTR?"

"I like variety too much for that," I replied. "I just don't seem to be satisfied with one. To tell you the truth as far as I'm concerned the more the merrier. I got my start in man sex at an interstate rest stop. It was nasty, superficial and just sex. It was also hot as hell!"

All this talk about sex got me going again. I got Lonnie to sit on my cock and we continued our conversation. My second trip up Lonnie's love canal was a revelation. I had fucked him for a solid half hour, but his ass was just as tight as it had been before. It was hard not to believe he was a virgin. He took his time to impale himself, but he had a slightly crazed look of determination on his face.

I'm no fool. I knew Lonnie was a calculating user, but once my cock was more than halfway in his hole, he lost his ability to think straight. That's happened to me a few times when the rush of sexual sensations totally overwhelms any other thoughts. When it happened to me, it was on a purely social occasion. This was business for me and I'm afraid I took advantage of Lonnie's vulnerability.

We talked as he bounced around on my cock. Every time Lonnie almost got his wits back, I'd give him a hard thrust and he go back to cock heaven. Lonnie was a farm boy from rural Indiana with the sex drive of a rutting bull. He got out of Indiana as soon as he could and his job at the Mandrake club was his ticket to the big time. He liked associating with the great and powerful.

He wasn't the brightest bulb in the hardware store, but he discovered his boyish looks and sex drive made up for that. He was paid for his extra services, but he really liked it when he got an invitation to go sailing, or to a party. One man was paying him to go to college. He liked most of the men he slept with. "Even if I don't, how bad can a blow job be?" he asked.

"Are most of the guys who work at the club pretty boys like you?" I asked.

Lonnie nodded. "Everyone's like me except Tyrone. He was the yard man who took care of the heavy lifting," he explained. "He was old, maybe 45, or 50 and hung like Godzilla. His cock was like yours, but thinner. Some of the members like a trip on the wild side. Being fucked by a big, Black buck turned them on. Tyrone left a week ago and he is missed." Lonnie looked at me. He rotated his ass and moaned. I bounced my hips and my cock went deeper. Lonnie's eyes rolled back into his head. I had hit a new spot.

"There's a job opening if you want it," Lonnie said when he came back to earth.

"Do you think a redneck, hillbilly love stick can replace your black horse cock?"

Lonnie looked at me again. "You look kind of scary and rough. I think they'd like that," he said. "It's the cock that counts, and that you have." I hadn't planned to start a career as a male hooker at a private men's club, but I saw some real advantages.

"How do I get the job?" I asked. "Is there an interview process?"

"I don't really know," he said. "I can find out." I gave him another hard bounce and we stopped talking shop. When he left, I gave him my phone number at a hotel. He said he'd call me the next day.

When I got back to the hotel, I gave Mr. Willamette a call and gave him the lowdown. I left out a few details. "I was thinking I'd try working there for a week or two and see if anything develops."

"Is something illegal going on there?" he asked.

"Something's going on," I said. "Legally it's misdemeanors at the most, but as a career killer, exposure would be the kiss of death."

"My son was involved?"

"He could have been involved, or he could have discovered something," I said. "Whatever it was, it was something big enough to justify murder."

Next morning Lonnie called. I went over to the club to meet the manager at 3:00 that afternoon. I thought I might brush up on my Southwest Virginia drawl, and then laughed to myself. I had the impression my accent had mellowed through the years, but that wasn't the way anyone else saw it.

The manager's name was Rutherford Mills, and he looked like a 1930's era lounge lizard. He didn't like my look at all. I was wearing a denim jacket. Under it, I had well-worn flannel shirt and even more worn jeans. When Rutherford saw the outline of my cock, his interest in me peaked. If you had a transcript of the meeting, you would have thought it was a normal job interview. Rutherford outlined the duties.

"To tell you the truth, Mr. Rutherford, I'll do whatever is needed," I said. "I've got no problem helping where help is needed."

He glanced at my cock again. "I like good attitude," he conceded. He hired me for a month probationary period. The salary was good, but not good enough to get an apartment in D.C. I asked if he knew of any apartments nearby. I hit the jackpot.

"If you want there are the old caretaker's rooms in the basement," Rutherford said. "It's just a small bedroom, sitting room and a half bath, but the price is right. You have to use the pool shower room."

"That sounds good to me," I said. "When do you want me to start work?"

"How about starting tomorrow morning?" I had a job.

The club occupied a big, Federal Style building in North West Washington. There was a small parking area in the rear and an elaborate, but overgrown garden next to it. Tyrone's strengths were genital, not horticultural. My Mom and her sister were picky on the subject of pruning and trimming, and on my first day I trimmed up some bushes. This was a success with the members. It originally had been a topiary garden and I discovered the lump of foliage was a topiary bird.

I also helped an elderly man get his Lincoln Town Car out of the parking area. I have no problems with tight parking lots. My mom also taught me to call older men "Sir," and to be helpful. That helped me make friends quickly. Tyrone had an attitude the members didn't appreciate. I looked so different from the rest of the staff; they all knew me by sight.

On my third day there, I interrupted a mugging on the street in front of the club. One of the neighbor ladies was walking her dog at 6:30 in the morning. I was on my way to sweep the sidewalk and walked right into it. I bellowed, "What the fuck is going on!" and then tackled him before he knew what was going on. Somehow, he managed to break a leg as he tried to escape. He woman's dog was a feisty Pekingese and did his best to relieve the mugger of his nose. It was a satisfactory interlude for the dog and me.

The police were happy too. The mugger had been a problem. I almost got my picture in the paper, but I told the reporter I had some woman problems back home and it would be best if I kept a low profile. I suggested the attack of the killer Pekingese might be a better story. The dog, Puffball, appeared with a photograph of the mugger and his bandaged nose on the front of the local section of the Post.

While I was getting along well with the members the same didn't apply to the staff. The boys who waited tables seem to think I was an alien from another planet. No members had asked me for any special favors yet, but I had been wearing my older jeans. My Mom always said you shouldn't put on display what's not for sale. She spoke with respect to women's clothing. The wear pattern on my jeans made it clear what I was packing. My jeans clearly showed the outline of my cock, balls and even my cock head were clear. I got glances, but no takers until after the mugging.

Grime and the mugger's blood covered me after the mugging, so I had to take a shower during regular club hours. Normally I was in the shower before or after the regular times of operation. Several club members took long showers while I cleaned up and we talked. They hadn't known I was living in the basement and I let slip my schedule for showering. I spent the rest of the day pruning. The garden was slowly getting in shape.

The club had bedrooms for the members' use on the upper floor. Several lived out of town and used them when they were visiting. One Senator and one Congressman were regular residents. The rooms had their own baths, so I didn't see the residents on the lower level of the building, unless they were swimmers.

That night, when the pool and exercise facility closed at 10:30 and I went to take a shower. I was sure someone would show up, but was wondering when it might happen. The place was empty when I got there, but a few minutes after I turned on the shower someone came in. I didn't recognize the man.

"Is there room for another guy in here?" he asked in a thick Southern accent. He was from the Deep South, maybe Mississippi, or Alabama.

"There sure is," I answered, "Are you finishing a late exercise session?"

"I don't seem to have hot water in my shower upstairs," he said. "Are you the new guy who got the mugger this morning?" I nodded.

"The name is Noland. I'm the new gardener." I washed my hair so he could get a good look at me.

"I'm Johnson," he said. He was wearing a towel when he came in the room. He hung it up, and took a showerhead across from me. Johnson was a tall, beefy, young man, maybe forty. He looked as if he had been an athlete. He had a gut, but made some effort to stay in shape.

"Damn, I thought I was hairy," he said. "You take the cake."

"We all get the cards we're dealt," I said. "I was short changed in the size division, but God must have doubled up on the body hair. It's either that, or I'm the missing link between men and apes."

"Hair isn't the only thing God doubled up on," he said.

I laughed. "You noticed?" I said. "I had an Uncle who said if I was naked all the time, I'd be the most popular guy in town. He had the same cock I have, but he married a woman who had many headaches. Sometimes life ain't fair."

"It looks like something you'd find in a museum of medical oddities," he said. He was laughing.

"When I die, I may give it to science," I replied. "As of now, I like my cock attached and in working order. I'm getting old, but there's a lot more fun left in it."

"You aren't the shy type, are you?" he asked, I looked at him and saw his cock was firming up. I smiled.

"I don't seem that shy anymore. We all have the same equipment. We all know how it works," I said. "You're looking good too." His cock was at half-staff and getting harder. Johnson blushed. "It's nice to know every thing's in working order." I turned off the water and dried off. Johnson looked as if he was at a loss of what to do next.

"I was thinking of having a night cap before bed," I said. "Would you like to join me in my ultra stylish in-town apartment?"

"I thought you had a room in the basement," Johnson said.

"It's all in the way you look at it," I replied. He smiled and followed me to my rooms. My window air conditioner was making an ineffectual effort to cool the room. I dropped my towel and made drinks. "Is

Bourbon and water okay for you? I have a bottle of Old Crow." He said sure. He kept his towel on, but there was no way for him to hide his excitement.

Johnson took a quick gulp. "It's odd to be having a drink with a naked guy," he said. "It's never happened before to me."

"Believe it or not, it happens to me quite a bit," I said. "Most guys are naturally curious, and most guys are really curious about cocks, especially when they are big, like mine."

"Does that bother you?"

"Nah, it's natural," I said. "It comes with the territory. There are two kinds of men in the world. Those who are interested in big cocks and those who are interested and pretend they aren't. Which are you?"

Johnson looked panicked for a second then said, "The later I'm afraid. Damn it's big!"

"That's more like it," I said. "Just relax and go with the flow." Johnson was sitting down and I was standing. I stepped closer to him and peeled back the skin, exposing my cock head. He leaned forward. I stepped closer. I was getting hard by now. That did nothing to reduce my cock's appeal.

"I've never done this before," Johnson whispered.

"Well, you're lucky to be starting at the top," I said. He didn't suck me at first. He kissed it and then flicked his tongue on the bloated gland.

"What should I do now?" he asked.

"I was hoping you would just relax," I said. I got on my knees, opened his towel and deep throated his organ. He must have shot off a year or two's supply of cum. Ejaculation followed ejaculation until he completely drained his balls. I took it all.

Johnson was weeping. "I'm sorry I didn't mean to do that," he cried.

"I loved every drop of it," I said. He leaned forward and took my cock in his mouth. When I started to shoot, he sucked on it like a baby at his mother's breast. I've always thought mutual orgasms are a good way to break the ice.

Part 2

Johnson stayed an hour and he knew a lot more about man sex when he left than when he came. He was 43 years old and had the sexual sophistication of a 13-year-old boy. His folks brought him up in a strict Baptist home, sent him to a Christian School and then he went to a born-again college. He fell for it, hook, line and sinker. By avoiding anything remotely like a normal life, he escaped dealing with real life situations.

He saved himself for marriage. Johnson married a virgin and they had one child. That had been an ordeal for both. When he got into Congress, it was a good opportunity to leave his wife at home and avoid a normal sexual relationship. He told me she was more relieved than he was. His ideas about sex would have made the Virgin Mary seem like Gypsy Rose Lee.

I think his puritanical ideas and high moral tone were due primarily to his sexual interest in men. He couldn't admit he was gay to himself, so he just got holier and holier. He told me he had never really looked at a naked man before he saw me in the shower room.

"Not even in the locker room at college?" I asked.

"I spent the whole time trying to avoid seeing their cocks," Johnson said. "I was on the football team at college, but the coach kept an eagle eye on the goings on in the locker room. We had curtains between the stalls. I worked hard at not looking down."

"Not even a glimpse?" I asked. "You're welcome to look now."

"Only as a boy," he said. "I've never seen an adult male naked. Christi thought it was all gross. I shaved off all my body hair to make her happy, but it didn't work."

"You're hairy now."

"Since I came to Washington, I let it grow back. She only comes to visit," he explained. "I didn't know that real men had sex together," he whispered. "I thought gays were all like the transvestites you see on television." He shifted so he could take a closer look at my cock, up close and personal. I had been soft, but the attention got me hard again, Johnson liked that a lot.

"Most of my friends are, if anything, macho to a fault," I said. "We're guys who help each other out. Cocks are the gifts that keep on giving."

"I thought it would be dirty. I was afraid of piss." Johnson said. "I hadn't thought of sex after a shower."

"When you get hard, you turn off the connection to your bladder and switch to your balls and prostate," I explained. "I was uneasy with stuff that comes from your cock, but that's water under the bridge now. I love cock juices. They mean my partner is revved up and ready to bogie."

Johnson looked up at me uncertainly. I leaned over and sucked his cock again. He was still drooling precum and it tasted sweet. "I'd better get back to my rooms," he said.

"Drop by again," I said. "I'm always here." I guessed he was having a guilt attack, but knew he would be back. I went to sleep. When I woke the next morning, I went to the shower early and two men came to check me out. One was an in shape sixty-year-old man called the Admiral. He was with a younger man, who I took as an aide.

The Admiral was blond, stocky and covered in curly reddish fur. I knew it must have taken a lot of work to stay in condition at his age. He had the body type that would naturally turn to fat easily. The aide was a crew cut military type, very muscular and hairless. They came in the shower and flanked me on each side. The aide tried to avoid looking at me, but the Admiral was frankly interested.

"Are you the guy who got the mugger yesterday?" he asked.

"That's me." I said, "They call me Noland."

"You don't look like much," he observed, "It must have been a small mugger."

"He was regulation sized. I'm small, but I'm mean and feisty," I said. "Most guys don't notice me until it's too late." The Admiral had a compact set of balls and cock, all about the same size. I washed my cock for a while to see how he would react. He firmed up nicely.

"You're full of surprises, aren't you?" he said as he looked at my growing cock.

"We all have the same equipment, just different shapes and sizes." I said. "I may have gotten the Lincoln Town Car of cocks, but they all get you to the same place. As far as I can tell, they all work the same." The Admiral was hard now and not at all worried. The Admiral had good gaydar. This was not his first gay encounter.

He looked at me and smiled. "Somehow you get more attractive as I get to know you better," he said as he stared at my cock. "I would have guessed you are more like a Hummer, than some luxury vehicle."

"Lots of guys like my mind," I replied. "It happens all the time."

The Admiral smiled. "Jack, come here and take a look at this," the Admiral said, calling his aide. "This boy's got a prize winner." I looked at Jack. Jack was embarrassed, but he already was erect. He relaxed when he saw the Admiral's hard cock.

"Have you ever seen a big one like that, Jack?" he asked. "It would split you in half."

"I've never split a guy in half yet," I said. "The world is filled with curious men. Most are lookers, but others want something more intense. You'd be surprised where it fits. Where there's a will, there's a way, especially if a man has good attitude. Are you into it?"

"I see you've had some experience," the Admiral said. "I know my limits. Jack on the other hand I think has an itch neither he nor I can quite scratch. You know that sort of itch you can't quite reach."

We heard two men talking as they came into the locker room and our conversation ended. I had to get to work, so I left. I figured the Admiral and his pal would reappear shortly.

The dog story hit the news that morning. It was a hit and the dog soon made it to national news. The neighbors on the street knew the real story and they slipped cookies and brownies to me. I had a busy day in the garden and one of the members asked if I could do some work on the side. He had an overgrown garden at his house in the suburbs. I told him I might be able to do something on Saturday. He casually mentioned he was Johnson's friend.

Oddly, some of the staff still steered clear of me. I admit I'm not everyone's ideal of a dreamboat, but I was puzzled. I also knew there were some club members who simply wouldn't speak with the staff unless they were giving an order. They seemed to be incapable of ordinary civility.

Most of the wealthy people I knew always framed their orders as requests. A lady would ask, "Could you bring us some coffee, Mary?"

Mary would of course respond, "Yes ma'am."

Several members of the Mandrake club ordered, "Get me a gin and tonic." It struck me as odd. I noticed many of these men were young and aloof. It seemed even odder to have these somewhat rude men in an elite social club. My image of an English social club is of almost suffocating politeness. That did not describe the Mandrake club.

That evening, I went to a small local restaurant for dinner. When I returned, I found Jack, the Admiral's aide waiting by the door to my room.

"Nice to see you gain," I said. He nodded and glanced around nervously. I got the impression he was afraid someone would see him. "Come on in and take a load off," I said. Jack came in. He relaxed the second he was out of sight.

"I hope I'm not bothering you?" he said.

"No problem," I replied, "Are you here on your own dime or representing the Admiral? I noticed he tends to speak for you."

"A little of each," Jack said. "Admiral Mc Hugh is helping my career and pushing me to get promoted. He's good for my career." He paused, and then resumed talking. "The sex thing isn't part of that," he whispered. "It just sort of happened."

"It sure seemed like part and parcel of your career advancement this morning."

"I guess it did," Jack admitted. "Somehow he found out I was gay. Instead of kicking me out, he had me assigned to his staff. You see he likes to watch. He almost never touches me sexually."

"That must be a bit uncomfortable for you," I said. "I'm a doer, not a watcher. It doesn't seem right to watch when you have a perfectly good cock an arm's length away."

"It was odd at first," Jack admitted. "I ran into one of Admiral McHugh's former aides, an Officer named Bill. He was a good man. Bill told me McHugh was on the up and up. He said it wasn't blackmail. He has never betrayed any of his aides."

"The Admiral is a nice guy with a quirk?"

Jack smiled. "That covers the bases well. He is a good officer too, intelligent and imaginative. It's strange, but he seems to know more about what I like sexually than I do," Jack said. "I'm turned off by hairy men. I like smooth, younger men. He found this hairy Italian Marine and got him to screw me. I was pissed, but it turned out to be the best sex I ever had. The Admiral liked it too. He told me it was a hand's free orgasm for him."

"That's why he wants me?"

"He heard about you from a friend. They mentioned your horse cock, but not how ugly and hairy you are," Jack said. "The minute he saw you I knew what he would want."

"You're afraid?"

"Sort of," he admitted. "You're just about everything I physically dislike in a man. I know you're a nice guy, and brave, but physically you're a turn off."

"You sure got hard in the locker room," I observed.

"That's exactly what the Admiral said," Jack exclaimed. "He says my cock knows what I really want."

"I guessed that too," I said. "Maybe your Admiral and I are on the same wave length. You don't need to worry though. I don't shove my cock into where it isn't wanted. You don't need to worry."

"It's not that simple," Jack said. "The more I think about you and that monster you call a cock, the more I want it. It's as if I'm a moth attracted to a flame. The Admiral says I'm like a stallion that needs to be broken in. Can you take your time? I think if you fuck me slow, I can do it."

"What makes you think I will do it at all?"

"Don't worry," Jack said. "McHugh will pay more than the going rate." That comment caught me by surprise, but I didn't let Jack know it. Lonnie provided extra services for pay, but I had the impression he was freelancing. I thought the prostitution was a small home business, not a large operation with a price list. I was curious as to whom the Admiral would pay, and if there was there a pimp's percentage. I wanted to ask Jack, but I didn't want him to know how little I knew.

"All you need to do it tell me when it hurts too much and I'll stop," I said. "The Admiral isn't into pain, is he?"

"Not at all," Jack said. He said he had to go, but he thought the Admiral would contact me shortly. I went out for a walk and made a call on my cell phone to Mr. Willamette.

"Do you know the name of your son's commanding officers?" I asked. "I only need to know the more recent ones."

"He was attached to the Joint Chiefs for the last year," Mr. Willamette said. "Before that he was almost five years with Admiral McHugh. That was a good time for William. He told me McHugh was a good man and he had learned a lot."

"That's the information I needed," I said. "Thanks." I returned to the club. The night parking attendant hadn't shown up, so I covered for him. The backup attendant would replace me at 10:00. Admiral McHugh drove in at nine.

"Jack said he talked to you earlier?" he asked. "You're with the program?"

"It's a little different, but I'm okay."

"I was hoping some variety wouldn't bother you," he said. "I hope Jack has no physical limitations. I'd like to see how far he could go. Room 8 is available. Is tonight at 11:00 good for you?" The club had seven rooms in the main building. Room 8 was in a former carriage house to the rear of the garden. It was very private. I had seen Lonnie going into it with one of the older members. I can put two and two together.

"My bedroom's good enough for me, if that's okay with you," I said. McHugh said it was fine with him; he didn't like to use Room 8 any more than he needed. McHugh arrived a little early and Jack arrived exactly on time. The Admiral had a drink or two, Jack had more than a few drinks. He wasn't drunk, but he was relaxed. That was good for me, but even better for him.

"By the way, I'm in charge here. I know I'm just an employee at the club, but when it comes to my cock, I run things. You understand?" I said.

"I understand," the Admiral said. I noticed Jack didn't even consider offering his opinion.

"Would a few politely phrased suggestions bother you?" McHugh asked.

I smiled. "Not a problem," I said. "Jack, I don't know if you're a no pain, no gain man, but if it hurts, let me know. I'm a fucker, not a sadist." Jack nodded. I started taking my clothes off. Jack followed suit, but the Admiral held back.

"I've seen your stuff, so don't get shy on me," I told him. "If this goes well, there will be precum and sperm all over the place. Save yourself some dry cleaning."

"I guess you're right about that," he conceded. The Admiral stripped.

"Man sex is one of those things that feels a lot better than it looks," I said as I steered Jack to my bed. Jack was middle height and in good shape. He had black hair and pale white skin. He was one of those people who burn and don't tan. He didn't show any sign of emotion, but his cock was already dripping precum. It was plentiful and sweet.

"Do you want to lube him up?" I asked the Admiral.

"You do it all," he said.

I coated my finger in lubricant and got Jack to put his legs up on the edge of the bed and spread them wide. His asshole was fully exposed. "I love fucking men, but I've never thought assholes were pretty. They feel good, but they just aren't pretty," I said as I began to lubricate him. I was going to take my time. "Your hole is pretty, Jack. It's a real surprise when I fuck men for the first time and they discover the ass is a sex organ. It's not as good as the cock though. It's best when the ass is tight, but then it's hard to get in."

I had been circling my finger around the hole with the cool lube. I then pushed a finger past the sphincter. Jack winced, and then moaned. "You're nice and tight, Jack," I said. I collected some of his drooling pre cum and used it to lubricate a second finger. He resisted my fingers until I found his prostate. I got a finger on each side of the small nut and had some fun with Jack. "Ass sex can be messy, but when it's good, it's really good," I said to the Admiral. "Jack's hole is tight, so it may take some time to open him up."

"Don't hurt him," the Admiral said. There was real concern in his voice. I think he was uneasy perhaps he was forcing Jack to do more than he could. Jack had tight buns and a small hole. I was fully erect and looking good. It looked as if it would be impossible to get my entire cock into Jack's ass. His sphincter clamped tightly on my fingers.

I pulled the finger out and coated my cock with lubricant. Then I nudged the cock head into Jack's ass. I didn't push. I just held it tightly against the hole. Jack shivered. I began to push, treating Jack's ass like a trampoline.

"If you could add some lube to my meat when I need it, it would be helpful," I said to the Admiral. I held Jack's legs in the air and spread them wide, so he had no natural defenses. A friend of mine had given me some pure amyl nitrate in ampules. I got the Admiral to hold Jack open, while I opened the ampule. I held it to Jack's nose. He inhaled and then I took a snort myself. The amyl hit my nervous system and a few seconds after it hit Jack. His sphincter lost all ability to resist. My cock slipped deep into Jack's quivering body. The Admiral moaned as he watched my cock disappear. Jack was winded but happy.

I stayed still for a while then made short pulsing motions. When Jack could breathe again, his body shivered and twitched a few times. He suddenly relaxed and I knew my cock had hit the right place. I began to make deep thrusts, almost pulling out and then going into the hilt.

"Damn, that's fucking beautiful," McHugh said. "Fucking beautiful."

Part 3

I suspected Jack would be sore the next day, but as for this night, he was one happy camper. It was more than he expected and much more than I expected. He was a reserved and careful man, but once I broke through that, he was your basic everyday sex pig. He loved it. I loved it and the Admiral loved watching it.

Admiral McHugh was the first to pop. I was pounding away at Jack's ass when several volleys of man seed spurted across Jack's torso. I don't know if he had been saving up, but it made a good show. I used some of it to re lubricate my cock. The Admiral liked that too.

Jack shot off next, so I pulled out. Much to my surprise, Jack had a short recharge time. He was ready to go again ten minutes later, so I did him doggy style. That too was a success. The Admiral had to go home to his wife, but Jack stayed for a third orgasm. I went to bed and slept well.

The next day I decided to check out Room 8. It was in a badly overgrown part of the garden, so it was easy enough to get near it without being seen. Once I was in the thicket, I was invisible from the club itself. I was working there when Lonnie went in with one of the older members. They came out an hour later. Lonnie came up to me.

"You really don't need to do this. It's kind of nice to be secluded," he said.

"Secluded I like," I said. "But I don't like places for a mugger to hide."

"I guess you're right about that," he admitted.

"I'll leave it nice, don't worry," I said. About an hour later, the manager came out. He too was worried I'd over prune. I had a section done and he thought it was acceptable. Another couple came by that afternoon and used the room. Just before they arrived, the manager came by and disappeared to the rear the building housing Room 8.

He had that slightly furtive look you have when you're trying to slip away to take a leak behind a bush. That seemed unlikely to me, so later that day I went sleuthing. There was a well-worn path to a camouflaged door. It looked old, but had a new lock and hardware on it. There was also new telephone line. I decided I'd check that out when it was dark.

While I worked in the garden, someone was nice enough to leave five hundred dollars in mixed bills in my room. The Admiral appreciated me. I also found out that my friend, Johnson, was actually W. Johnson Rutter III, an up and coming congressman. That evening I went wandering around Georgetown and North-West Washington. I'd been there before but never had the time to explore. It was dark when I got back to the club. I went into the garden and went to Room 8.

The lights were on in the room, so I went to the rear. The door was locked, but I had some skills picking locks. It wasn't anything fancy and I was inside after a minute or two of work. The room had a computer and monitor. The monitor showed the bedroom. A tool bar on the screen showed monitors One through Six. Room 8 was bugged. I left quickly and went to my room.

I was wondering if Johnson, Jack, or the Admiral would show up that night in the shower. None of them did. A man I had never seen before appeared. He was tall and thin, about 30 to 35. He had a hairy chest and a pronounced treasure trail connecting to his pubic hair. The man was obviously nervous. I saw him peeking at me from the locker room. He finally got enough nerve to join me in the shower.

"It's good to end the day with a nice hot shower," I said.

"It sure is," he said. "Are you a member here?"

"Nope, I'm the yard guy, Noland," I said. "I live in a small apartment in the back."

"Are you the guy who caught the mugger?"

I nodded.

"You're kind of famous here," he said. "Everyone's talking about you." He looked at me. "They said you're hairy as ape."

"Is that a problem?" I asked.

"Not really," he said. He paused and then said, "Actually, not at all."

I smiled at him. "Did they mention anything else about me?"

The young man looked at my cock and smiled. "Well there was one other thing they mentioned."

I laughed, "You'd be surprised how many guys notice it," I said as rinsed off my cock. "Is it what you expected?"

"They didn't mention you were uncut," he said. "I've not seen many uncut guys this close."

"Let me guess, that isn't a problem either," I said, laughing.

"Not a problem at all." I hope I haven't insulted you," he said.

"What's your name?"

"Conrad," he said. "My Dad's a member here."

"I was thinking you are a bit young for this place," I said. Conrad was still looking at my cock. I turned off the shower. Poor Conrad looked disappointed. "My room's in the back. Come by if you want to," I whispered to him.

"Now?"

"Sure, I've got nothing to do tonight," I said. We dried off; I put on my bathrobe and went to my room. Three or four minutes later, he knocked on the door. I let him in.

"Are you sure I'm not bothering you?" he asked.

"Don't worry. I don't mind some company. I'm new in town," I said. "Would you like a beer?" he said yes.

I was still wearing my bathrobe and it wasn't too securely fastened. He pretended he wasn't looking.

"I don't know why I'm here," he muttered.

"Well I'm pretty sure I know why you're here," I said. "Lots of men are curious. There's nothing wrong with being interested in a big cock. It seems to be a part of human nature."

"You aren't offended?"

"Shit no," I replied. "You have a much better chance of offending a guy for mentioning he has a mini cock, than admiring a horse cock like mine." I stood up and took my robe off. "Feel free to take a good look."

Conrad was unsure what he should do, but curiosity and desire got the better of him. He leaned closer to look.

"Is it the uncut cock you are interested in, or the size?" I asked.

He looked up at me. "Do I have to make a choice?" he asked.

I laughed. "No, it seems to be a package deal anyway," I said. "You have to take the cock as it is and I throw in the balls and ball sack for free." He laughed and relaxed some. "If you want to see the cock head, you're going to have to peel the skin back."

"I can touch it?"

"Go right ahead," I told him. He reached over gingerly and touched my cock. He relaxed a little more. I wondered if he was expecting a lightening bolt form the sky when that happened. "I feel odd about this," he said. "Are you going to get hard?"

"If I'm lucky, I will," I replied. "Let me warn you. It doesn't get any smaller when it's hard." Conrad laughed again, and then he peeled the skin back exposing half of my cock head. "It's really shiny," he whispered. "It's big too."

"It feels really good when you pull the skin back and forth over the head," I said. As he stroked it, I got hard. Getting hard never lessens my allure. Conrad was getting into it.

"You've got some nice equipment yourself," I said. "Why don't you pull it out and we can have some real fun?"

"I don't know if I want to do this," he said in an unconvincing manner.

I laughed. "Let me tell you, you'd be a lot more convincing if you weren't stoking my cock," I said.

He looked up at me and smiled. "I guess you're right about that," he admitted. "It's so big. I've never seen a cock like yours. It's just that I've never really done this before. I'm not sure what I should do."

"I could be accused of some self interest in this, but you may not run into another cock like mine in a long while," I said. "You'll regret not giving it a try. Gather ye rosebuds while ye may."

"What do you want me to do?" he asked.

"Why don't you get more comfortable and we'll let nature take its course?"

There was a brief battle between reserve and lust and lust won. Conrad stripped. As I expected he was hard as a rock and his slit glistened with precum. I dropped to my knees and began to suck him. After a minute or so we went to my bed and sixty-nined. He was much taller than I was, but it worked out. He was good at it. I was pretty sure this wasn't his first time. I ooze precum at a good rate and he had no problem with that at all.

After a while, we calmed down. "We're going at this like locomotives with a full head of steam," I said. "I'm going to pop soon. If you have some time, we can slow down and make it last."

"I've nothing planned for the rest of the night," Conrad said. "We can take it easy. I hate to sound superficial, but your cock is beautiful. It turns me on big time. It's like a magnet." We talked for a while. Conrad would take a lick every time it looked as if I was losing my erection.

"You've got a lot of experience?" he asked.

"I've had my share. Some guys are just lookers, others are really into it," I answered. "You're into it more than you want to admit."

"Can you tell?" he asked. "I was hoping it didn't show. If my dad found out, it would kill him."

"Don't worry. It doesn't show. As I said, I've been around," I explained. "Is your Dad the conservative type?"

"Hell, he's an Admiral and all his friends are hard-assed military types," Conrad said. "You can ask anyone. They'll tell you Admiral McHugh is the most straight-laced man in the Navy." Fortunately, I was licking his cock, so he didn't see the expression on my face when he dropped that bombshell.

"Is he a good father?" I asked.

"No one believes me when I tell them, but yes," Conrad said. "I'm in the State Department. When I didn't go the military path, everyone thought he'd blow a gasket, but he was fine with it." He licked my cock again. "Do you fuck guys with this?" he asked.

"I sure do," I replied. "Are you volunteering?"

"I'm interested in it, but you're out of my league," he said. "I've topped a few times, but bottoming wasn't much of a success."

"You liked the top?"

"It was good for me, but my partner thought I was too big," Conrad said. "God knows what he would have said if he saw you!"

"As I said you've got some nice equipment," I said. "Nice curve too. It might be a good fit."

"You bottom?" Conrad asked. He was on my bed. I moved and got Conrad on his back. I suddenly straddled him, got his cock at my hole and sat back. I had been sucking him, so he was spit lubricated. It was a good fit. Conrad was a thick seven inches. It wasn't a challenge, but I definitely knew I had a cock stuck up my ass. I was hoping the curve would do something exciting, but it missed the hot spot. Conrad was shocked when I sat on his cock, but adjusted quickly.

I squeezed my buns and rotated my ass. "Can you do that again?" he moaned. I did a little hula dance on his cock. I think his cock grew larger, and then slipped into the groove. His hard, curved cock found the spot.

"Am I fucking you, or are you fucking me?" Conrad asked.

"Boy, I don't think it makes any difference who is doing what to whom," I said. It was great. I don't bottom much, but when I do, I'm an active bottom. Conrad provided the cock. My ass did the stimulating. I got it so every time I twitched, his knob made direct hit on my prostate. It was hard to do, but when he gave my nut a sperm bath, I popped like a Roman candle. I coated his hairy torso with man cream. A good time was had by all.

Conrad left, and I went to bed. Before I fell asleep, I decided to see if I could find the other end of the telephone lines coming from the cameras in Room 8. It was possible the cameras were intended for a voyeur's personal pleasure, but it seemed more likely they were for a blackmailer's use. I didn't know where Jack, the Admiral, Congressman Rutter, or Conrad McHugh fit in the Washington establishment. All liked man sex and all had careers at risk if someone exposed their sexual preferences.

It was Saturday, so I had the day off. I was going to go back to Richmond and see what was up at the office, but there was a small grease fire in the kitchen. The Club's traditional, old-fashioned breakfasts' were popular. That meant bacon and sausage in great abundance. The grease overwhelmed the poor range hood. It wasn't a big fire, and the sprinkler in the hood extinguished the blaze, but it made a mess. This was a good opportunity for me to get some gossip from the staff.

Most of the maintenance crew was off for the weekend, I was willing to do the clean up with the kitchen staff. I was scrubbing the soot-covered kitchen cabinets when the manager came in; he looked over the work and went home, leaving the assistant manager in charge. The assistant manager was a twenty-three-year-old kid. He was clueless and a bit officious. He tried to tell me what to do. It told him let me do it my way, or do it himself. It was an easy decision for him.

His name was Carlton, and he did go out, got us cleaning materials, and later got lunch. It turned out he was willing to help. He just didn't have any experience doing anything physical. I was working with Roosevelt, the headwaiter, and Louis, one of the chefs. Roosevelt and Louis were good men and had been at the club a long while. Roosevelt was an older black man who knew where the skeletons are buried. He was also a gossip. I couldn't have asked for more.

It didn't take me long to realize Roosevelt, Louis and Carlton were gay, but they weren't the right type for the club members. They seemed to be interested observers. "The club has changed since the new manager came," Roosevelt said. "He seems to have brought in new members who aren't as distinguished as the older ones."

"A few of the guys are a bit rough around the edges," I said.

"You're a strange one to be noticing that," Carlton said.

"He's right," Roosevelt replied. "There are some odd things going on like Commander Willamette's murder. We've never had a member murdered before."

"Was he one of the new members?" I asked.

"He was new, but he seemed to be a nice guy," Carlton said. "He was very pleasant and affable. Some of the members are too elevated to say hello to an assistant manager. He wasn't one of those."

"He was a real gentleman, young, but of the old school," Roosevelt said. "He took up with Earnest Hatfield, who is definitely not a gentleman. I thought it was odd. Commander Willamette was very distracted the weeks before he was murdered. I thought something was wrong."

"Did you say anything to the police?" I asked.

"There was nothing to say. Feelings aren't facts," Roosevelt said. "The manager and Hatfield are thick as thieves."

"When you add in Paul DeBoer, you have the terrible trio, the bane of my existence here," Carlton said.

"How so?" I asked.

"Rude, unreasonably demanding and nasty sums them up," Carlton said. "I'm an underling here and they seem to look for ways to drive me crazy."

"They aren't a problem for me," Roosevelt said. "They're too scared of black men to say anything to me!"

"You're lucky. DeBoer and Hatfield are pleasant in direct proportion to your rank and potential for helping them get their way," Carlton said.

"That's it!" Roosevelt exclaimed, "That's what bothered me about Hatfield's friendship with Willamette. Willamette was too low ranking to be of assistance to him. I couldn't figure out what was up. It didn't make any sense."

"What is Hatfield's day job, other than being a jerk?" I asked.

"I don't really know. He puts on airs and pretends to be a spy, bit that is a fantasy. He's a bit too obvious to be a real agent. I think he likes James Bond too much. Hatfield is wealthy and well connected with the ultra conservative group."

"Which one?" I asked.

"I'm not sure, they all sound alike," Roosevelt said.

"I don't understand DeBoer's room," Carlton said. "It has a separate lock and the Club staff is not allowed to clean it. He has his own people come in to do it. He's the only one in the club who has that arrangement."

"Is he a high-ranking official?" I asked. "Maybe he has secret files or documents."

"He works for some high toned think tank," Roosevelt said. "It's something like the All America Foundation, or some such thing. He tries to suggest he's CIA, but I've known a number of them. You never find out about the real ones until the funeral. You never suspect. He's putting on airs."

We cleaned up the kitchen by 3:00 so it was possible to do the prep for dinner that night. There was an important social event at 8:00 that evening. Soot and grime covered everyone who had done the cleaning and Carlton let everyone use the showers to clean up. Normally the members' exercise area was strictly off limits to staff. I was an exception since I lived in the basement.

I'm unimpressive fully dressed, but I shine when I'm naked and covered in running water. Roosevelt was impressive dressed, but naked he was in good shape and his black snake hung almost to his knees. Lou, the chef, was a beefy Italian who was almost as hairy as I was. He was uncut, with huge balls, but a modest cock. Carlton was pudgy and bland. When he saw Roosevelt and me, he got hard and stayed hard.

There was work to be done, so there was little time to do anything except admire. As the men went upstairs to get dinner made, Roosevelt whispered to me, "Damn, you're good for a white boy!"

"Sperm's always white." I replied. "If you have an interest, I'm always ready to trade. You don't mind trying out Redneck High Test?"

"If you don't mind Afro Love Juice, I'm game. Fresh, straight from the spigot?" he asked. I nodded. "By the way, Carlton is a bottom, a good one so I'm told," he added. Roosevelt and I understood each other.

Part 4

For the time being, I had an embarrassment of clues. I had a locked room and some unattractive suspects. Blackmail almost certainly was at the core of the scheme. I wasn't sure if money or power was the objective. I didn't know if Lonnie and his friends were involved, or if they were unwitting accomplices. I also didn't know if they had bugged or monitored my room.

Lonnie had mentioned Tyrone was the club top. I didn't know if he was serving the staff, or the club members. I hoped I wasn't on a DVD somewhere with the Congressman or the Admiral. There were too many options, none of them good.

After my first few days at the club, I had an oversupply of sexual partners and the potential for more. There were too many people and too many possibilities. No one dropped by that night so I had some solid thinking time. I was positive Commander Willamette had been murdered. He was a member of a Club that had a room wired for photographs and had a staff that was willing to satisfy a lonely, closeted gay man's sexual desires.

Johnson, the Admiral, Jack and Conrad were all deeply closeted and exposure would ruin their professional lives. They were also culturally conservative men who hadn't been able to deal with their sexual preferences. I knew Willamette was wealthy, but had no idea if the other men were any more than well off financially.

The video set up was elaborate. It was easy to envision someone like Lonnie trying to get some money from the men, but Lonnie was being paid for his services any way. When I spoke with him, he seemed to be satisfied with the arrangement. There was no way in hell he could have afforded the fancy computer recording system.

The club manager hadn't impressed me, but he seemed like a worker bee. I hadn't met DeBoer or Hatfield, but from Roosevelt's description, they were likely suspects. I would have to find some way to meet them. I got up early on Sunday morning and went on a long walk. I called into my office and asked them to look into DeBoer, Hatfield and the All America Foundation.

I went in a Starbuck's hoping an expensive cup of coffee would inspire me. I don't look like a Yuppie and I think I scared several of the patrons. "Do you have anything that has double the caffeine," I asked. The young woman recommended, "Mocha Java, this will grow hair on your chest," she remarked. Then she noticed the hair poking out of my shirt. "Sorry about that," she said when realized what she had said.

"It comes with the territory," I said. I sat at a table and was halfway through my cup when a loud drunk came in. It was 9:30 in the morning and a bit too early in my mind to be in that state. He wasn't a good drunk either. The young woman who had served me apparently was the manager that morning, and she went over to the man and politely asked him to leave.

She was nice, but firm. The drunk would have nothing of it. He fell against a table and hit one of the patrons. It was supposed to look like an accidental blow, but I wasn't sure.

"Time's up," I said in my deepest bass. "You're not welcome here and it's time to go." The man looked at me, sneered, and said, "Like hell!"

That was the last word he said in the Starbucks. I gave him a sucker punch, winded him, grabbed him by his belt and tossed him out on the street. A patrol car passed by and stopped. "Johnny, I told you to stay out of this area!" a Cop yelled from the car. The drunk ran like a bat out of hell.

"Are you okay, mister?" the cop asked. "Johnny runs a scam."

"Sure, I was just taking out the trash," I said. The cop went chasing Johnny.

I went back to my cup of coffee. "You get a free refill for that," the woman said. I also got a brownie that really hit the spot.

"I see you're up to your usual tricks," a voice said. It was the Admiral. "How are you doing this morning?"

"Just fine, feel free to join me," I said and motioned for him to sit at my table. He was with Jack and a tall man I didn't know. He was about the Admiral's age, but had a bushy, ginger colored beard. He introduced the man as Red. They joined me.

"Did kids pick on you as a child?" Red asked in a pronounced Scot's accent.

I smiled, "A few guys tried it once," I said.

"Never twice?"

"Once is one time too many as far as I'm concerned," I said. Red was a former officer in the Royal Navy and was now a consultant. We chatted for a while and the Admiral had to leave. I went to the men's room

Red appeared the men's room. "Are you the one Jack told me about?" he asked.

"I might be," I said, "I hope it wasn't something bad."

"It wasn't bad at all." Red replied. "He said there was a lot more to you than meets the eye."

"Are you a member of the club?" I asked.

Red looked shocked, "the Mandrake Club?" Red laughed. "Not enough money and not conservative enough to join that fine institution," he said. Leaning close to me he added, "I'm a dues paying member of another club. Perhaps you'd like to join Jack and me for lunch?"

"Sure, if Jack doesn't mind," I answered. I knew Jack wouldn't mind. Red had a room at the Watergate Hotel so we took a taxi.

Once we were in the room Red was all business. "This is my only free time this week, so I'd like to get as much R &R in as possible," he said.

"Are you a watcher, like the Admiral?" I asked.

"To tell you the truth, just watching strikes me as frustrating," Red said. "I'm a man of action." To underline that thought, he started to strip. "I'm not into love. I like sex, hard thrusting, ball busting sex. There's not much you can do with a cock and an arse that I don't like." We were all naked by then. He looked me in the eye. "Is Jack the only bottom here?"

"I tend to top, but I like it all," I said.

Red smiled. "That describes me too," he said. "I've not been popped in a while, so it may take some doing. Let's play it by ear."

Red said he was into sex, just sex and that was fine with me. It turned out the three of us really hit it off. Red was a good fucker, but he was a better lover. He liked his men young and he liked them hung. Jack and I were his dream come true. Red wasn't shy and was into ass holes, specifically Jack's hole.

Red's ginger beard was the same color as his body hair. He had the pink complexion you would expect of a red head. He had a good cock, average in length and a bit thicker than normal. He had balls that would have made a bull proud. His balls were true cum factories. I've often said good sex is messy. By that standard, we had damn good sex.

Since Red hadn't fucked Jack before, he went first. We got Jack on the edge of the bed. I held his legs wide open as I straddled his face. Jack had to choose between my balls and my cock. He alternated.

From this position, I could adjust the height of Jack's ass to meet Red's needs. Red spent a lot of time lubricating Jack's hole. Red seemed to be a believer in deep lubrication, so when it became time to replace his finger with his cock, it was effortless. Just because it was effortless didn't mean it was ineffective. As Red's cock slid into Jack's love tunnel, I felt Jack react.

Red penetrated quickly, but he stopped when he was fully embedded to give Jack a chance to get his bearings. I pulled Jack's legs toward me, and then released them a few times. This had the effect of massaging Red's cock. Jack was moaning now, so I knew it was good for him too. Much to my surprise, Red shot off. After he stopped spasming, he pulled out and we traded places.

Jack's ass was good and open. Red had already stretched his twitching hole and a mixture of lube and cum drooled from it. My cock entered like Moses crossing the Red Sea. The cream in his ass acted like ball bearings. I rarely get to poke an ass as open as Jack's. The experience was oddly relaxing, but still exciting.

Red had taken my place straddling Jack's face. Red's uncut, soft cock was still dripping. Jack was intercepting the drips with his tongue. I concentrated on Jack, deep fucking him with slow strokes. His ass was stretched wide when I was in, and didn't close all the way when I pulled out. When I pulled out, Red would pull Jack's legs toward him and lick his vacated ass. Then he tried to force his tongue into the hole.

I would then fuck Jack again. I noticed Red was now fully erect. Red and I tag fucked Jack for the next hour and a half. Red was inventive and during one of the rotations he sat on Jack's cock as I fucked Jack. In another Red fucked me as I did Jack. I shot off twice, but Red must have popped a half dozen times. In each orgasm, he sprayed us with his huge loads. I think Jack would have gone on for another hour, but Red believed in moderation in all things, enough was enough. You would think that three strangers screwing each other for over an hour would get repetitive and boring, but that wasn't a problem.

Red's taste for variety was helpful, but more important was the emotional feeling the long sessions created. Jack started the session as a willing ass, and ended up as a person. We all merged into a mutual stimulation and pleasure society. We found out each other's strengths and weaknesses. I was trying to see what I could do to make it better for Red and Jack. They were looking after my interests. It doesn't get any better than that.

During sex I'm normally 90% a horny, big dicked, man fucker and 10% a private eye, but that 10% is always present. During a lull in the passion, I found out the Admiral and Jack were in intelligence, and guessed Red was in the same line of work. Jack had an engineering background and had something to do with weapons' evaluation. He wasn't a spy or undercover, I guessed he was an analyst.

Jack had to go, so he took a shower and left, leaving me with Red. At first, I thought he just wanted more cock play, one on one. That was true, but he also had an interest in the Mandrake Club.

"How long have you been there?" he asked.

"Just a week," I replied. "It's not quite what I expected."

"How so?"

"It's an odd combination of people. Both the members and the staff seem mismatched," I said.

"More hookers than you expected?" Red asked.

"You do get around," I said. "It seems to be an odd combination of old money, arch conservative politics and Gay sex. I take it you have a connection inside."

"Not anymore," Red said.

"Commander Willamette?" I suggested. Red looked shocked for a split second, and then resumed his normal demeanor.

"Who exactly are you?" he asked.

"Let's just say, I'm interested in finding the Commander's murderer," I said. "That seems to involve prostitution and blackmail."

"You're not the Metropolitan Police?"

"I'm working for the Commander's father," I said. "He was unhappy with the Police response."

"Would you be interested in helping me out?" Red asked. "We can pay you well."

"I already have a job and money isn't a problem," I said. "If you spoke with Mr. Willamette, he could give you clearance."

"I'm not sure I can deal with a grief-stricken father."

"I wouldn't worry about that," I explained. "He would be happy knowing his son died an honorable death."

Red brightened up. "Actually, that is one thing I can do," he said. "The commander was a brave man." Red gave me his card and said he would be in touch. His name was Redfern DeLacourt, and he was the Senior Analyst for the British Technology Group. I went back to the club wondering exactly what was going on.

Two days later, I got a call from Mr. Willamette. "I got a visit from the first Secretary of the British Embassy and a Mr. DeLacourt this morning," he said. "It seems you are in a position to be helpful to them. You are free to keep them abreast of your investigations. Anyway you can help Mr. Delacourt is acceptable to me, but I trust your judgment on that."

I wanted to see Red, but I figured he'd get in touch with me in his own time. I was out walking in the early evening and getting my cell calls made. I called the office, but no one was in. I found a little pocket of slightly run down houses and apartments about six blocks from the club. It was an area associated with Georgetown or George Washington University students.

"What are you doing here?" a voice asked. It was familiar, but not quite recognizable. I looked around and saw Louis, the cook.

"An after work constitutional," I said. "Are you done with work already?"

"I sure am," Louis replied. "I was a baker for years. I am up at 4:30 and at work by 5:00 every morning. I'm done early too."

"You live here?"

"I've been here for 25 years," Louis said. "It was just expensive when I came here. I am the apartment manager in my spare time, so I get a deal on the rent. Would you like a cup of coffee or a beer?"

I agreed and went to his apartment. The coffee was good, but I was surprised when Carlton emerged from a bedroom, he was wearing only boxer shorts. He was more surprised.

"Are you friends?" I asked.

"We're friendly enough, but Carlton sublets a room and helps with the rent," Louis said. "I have to admit. We were impressed with you yesterday." I looked Louis in the eye and knew to what he was referring.

"I am a hard worker," I said, smiling. Both men laughed.

"I hope you don't think I'm superficial, but how in hell did a small guy like you get all that cock?" Louis asked.

"A friend of mine said that God has a sense of humor," I said. "Unfortunately, while I have a lot of cock, I'm also a top, so I don't have a place to put it often."

"Do I have a deal for you!" Carlton said. We all laughed.

"Lots of guys have bigger eyes than they have ass holes," I said. "My cock isn't for amateurs."

With that comment, Louis burst out laughing. He was all but rolling on the floor. "Amateur!" Louis exclaimed. "Carlton's 27 years old and he already has a lifetime achievement award."

Carlton looked insulted and then laughed. "I'm not that bad!" Carlton exclaimed. "I admit I've bottomed once or twice." His cock had already tented his boxers. Louis continued laughing.

"Carlton is the Energizer Bunny when it comes to getting fucked," Louis said. "Nothing is too big and no one fucks too long."

"I guess he makes friends easily?" I said.

"I'm willing enough," Carlton said, "but I'm not pretty enough." Carlton was about five feet seven and beefy. He wasn't fat, but he was no beach bunny. He looked young to me, but he wasn't like the boyish Lonnie. "I'm not too good at playing the blushing virgin either," Carlton added. "The men at the club like them fresh."

"They think Lonnie's a virgin?" I asked.

"Hard to believe, isn't it," Louis said. "Poor Carlton is a bit too vocal in his enthusiasm." Louis began unbuttoning his shirt. "Let's go to the bedroom." It would be good if I could resist temptation, but that isn't my strong suit. We went to the bedroom.

I usually have to get the men I fuck ready, but Carlton was hot to trot. Louis was into it too. He liked to watch and seemed to have in-depth knowledge of Carlton's sexual anatomy. I assumed most of his knowledge came through direct exploration. Louis was more than willing to give me detailed instructions.

Willing though he was, it was a tight fit. Carlton wanted it bad and was willing to take any discomfort necessary. Louis provided lube and encouragement. It took a good fifteen minutes to get it fully embedded in Carlton's ass. Once we were pubic hair to ass lips, Carlton got his breath.

Carlton twitched a few times and we were off to the races. He had remarkable control of his rectum. It was almost prehensile. Carlton massaged my cock as I rammed him. Nothing was too hard or rough for him. Once I was in his ass, Carlton had a sphincter of steel. He tried to grab my cock and hold it.

Part 5

I spent a good two hours with Carlton and Louis. We split the time between conversation and fornication. It was a good mix. I found out more about the locked room occupied by DeBoer. Most of the time he ate out, or in the Club's dining room, but once and a while he called for room service. He would ask that Paul, one of the younger waiters, bring up the food.

This excited Paul. He said they were good tippers. "DeBoer is usually a shitty tipper, so the money must come from a guest," Louis said.

"Are the guest's members of the club?" I asked.

"Not as far as I can tell," Carlton replied. "I don't know who they are. You're supposed to have guests register at the reception area, but his guests arrive with him, so we don't have their names. I did see one of his pals on the Sunday Morning talk shows, but I don't remember who it was."

I wanted to meet DeBoer, but I couldn't figure out how to do it. I was the outdoor man and DeBoer wasn't ever in the garden and didn't exercise. I knew what he looked like, but no more than that. Meeting him turned out to be easy. The manager solved my problem. He came up to me while I was working in the garden.

"Noland, we have a member who'd like to see you this evening," he said.

"Sure, what's his name?"

"No names are necessary," the manager replied. "You are to take a shower tonight at 11:15. That's all you need to do."

"That's easy enough," I said. The manager left.

I was at the shower room at the appointed time. DeBoer and another man appeared after a few minutes. DeBoer was a heavy man who always wore expensive suits. Suits can cover a multitude of sins, and DeBoer's body was sinful. He had poor skin tones, sort of a mottled grey-green. It looked as if he had melted. He had no cock. A fold of fat hid his genitals. I have often said I like any man as long as he has a cock. De Boer was lacking this feature.

His friend was an average guy, with military style moustache and a tan. He dyed his hair black, but his chest hair was salt and pepper. He joined me in the shower as DeBoer lurked in the locker room.

"Are you Tyrone's replacement?" the friend asked abruptly. "I'm the gardener, if that's what you mean," I replied. He looked me in the eye, then at my cock.

"I'm a top. Is that like Tyrone?" I asked. The man looked taken aback and then he smiled.

"I'm Carl," he said.

"Noland here," I said. "Is your friend a watcher?" Carl glanced at De Boer and DeBoer left the room.

"He just likes to help ease the way to true love," Carl said.

"To tell you the truth, I'm not much into true love," I said. "I'm not opposed to guys helping each other out, though."

"That's a start," Carl said. "Are you into wrestling?"

"My room's around the corner," I said. I soon found out Carl wasn't into wrestling. He was more into muggings. As soon as I got to my room, he jumped me from behind. He was much bigger than I was, and wasn't into any of the niceties of wrestling. He caught me by surprise. Carl was trying to pin my prostate with his cock.

I'm an open-minded guy when it comes to sex, but that stops when it comes to rape. I know some men do it as part of a role-playing exercise. They see it as being all fun. It's not fun for me. I've had others who were into spanking. Maybe it's good for them, but I think it just wastes time and takes longer to get to the real sex I have a strong aversion to men who like to fight with small guys.

Carl had me. After pinning my arms behind my back, and jabbering on about me being his fuck slave and man cunt, he got down to business. He had an average cock crowned with a big knob. Carl wasn't much of a leaker, so he was planning a dry fuck. I relaxed. He thought I had given up.

I discovered Carl wasn't much of a multi-tasker. He had to hold me down while staying hard and forcing my ass. As he tried to force my hole, he relaxed his hold on my arms. I was still a bit wet from the shower. One of my arms slipped free and I gave him a strong blow to his gut. He lost his grip on my other arm and it was all over for him. His fortunes changed in a few seconds.

When I catch a mugger, I like to administer a little in-the-field punishment. The judges back in Richmond coined a phrase a "Clydesdale Cast." I didn't want to break Carl's leg or arm, but I wanted him to know the errors of his ways.

When it was over Carl was chastened, humbled and royally fucked. I had him by the balls, the real balls, not the metaphorical balls. With a ball-crushing grip on his privates, he was under control. Any time he tried to resist, I squeezed hard and he twitched in agony.

I don't like dry fucks. I was feeling some regret I couldn't do unto him what he intended to do to me, but there is a God. Carl may not have been an ass virgin, but he was close. The Almighty had also seen fit to give Carl a very tight hole. That hole was five or six sizes bigger when I was done with him. There was only one problem. Carl had a raging hard-on the whole time and had a hand's free orgasm. He shot that all over my bedspread when it was over.

I sent him on the way, telling him, if he ever tried that again, it would be my fist up his ass the next time. When I said that, he ejaculated again. Carl was a piece of work. When I got up the next morning, I was listening to NPR on the radio when I heard Carl's voice. He was talking about moral renewal and the depravity of the modern America. The anchor ended the segment with, "That was Dr. Carl Montague of the All America Foundation."

Carl was one of those sanctimonious talking heads with a big, bad secret hidden deep in his psyche. On the radio he sounded self-confident and without the smallest suggestion of uncertainty. It was hard to believe it was the same man who whimpered as I pounded his ass hours earlier.

While I was sweeping the sidewalk that morning, Johnson came up to me.

"How's it going?" he asked.

"Things are always good for me," I replied. "And you?"

"A busy day on the Hill ahead, but good otherwise," he said. He got closer. "Are you going to have some free time tonight?" I nodded. As we talked, Jack came up to us. He was dressed in his naval uniform and looked good.

"Congressman Rutter," he said, "I'm Commander Fitzwilliam, Admiral McHugh's aide. I was hoping to talk with you about part of the Naval Appropriations bill that will be coming to you shortly."

"I've seen you around," Johnson said. "I'm filled up today, but anytime tomorrow will be fine." He paused. "Have you met our local hero, Noland? He's the mugger catching gardener."

"We've met," the Commander said.

"As a matter of fact, I think you both know me equally well," I said. "You share more common interests than you know." The Congressman looked puzzled and then caught on. They were both good looking men and I sensed an immediate attraction.

"Johnson was going to drop by to see me tonight," I said.

"Around ten," the Congressman added. They shook hands and went on their way. Both men were uneasy with their sexual preferences and I wasn't sure they would show up. I knew they wanted to, but might not have enough nerve.

That afternoon I saw Paul going to Room 8 with one of the members. A few minutes later another, younger man went to the room. He looked slightly familiar, but wasn't a member. After an hour the older man left, but Paul and the third man remained. I was working near the door when Paul peaked out. "Noland, can you come over here?" I went to him. "I've got a friend here. He's a bit of a size queen, would you mind doing a little show and tell?"

"I don't know about that," I answered.

"He's a nice guy," Paul said, "He's fun, not like the other guys."

"More pleasure than work?" I asked.

Paul leaned close to me. "Half the guys shoot before I get off, the other half can't get it up at all. Thompson's different. Everything's in working order. Can you come in and give him a show? Don't worry about the garden. The members come first."

I went in the room. There was a sitting area on the lower floor of the former carriage house, but we went up stairs to the bedroom. "Thompson, this is Noland, the yard man," Paul said.

"I noticed the garden was looking good," Thompson said. "You must be a hard worker. It has looked like crap for years." He was average in height, with sandy hair. He had delicate features and pale, blue eyes. He was good looking, if bland. I guessed he had been handsome as a young man.

My shirt was partially unbuttoned and my pelt was showing. "You're a hairy one," Thompson said. "Usually, I'm the fur ball." He unbuttoned his shirt. He was clean-shaven and manicured in appearance. His shirt hid a thick mat of curly, dirty blond hair. I unbuttoned the rest of my shirt. I was sweaty and dirty from the garden. I had a feeling that wouldn't bother Thompson at all.

He unbuckled his belt. Thompson was the kind of man who led by example. I liked that. I guessed he was a jogger. His body was lean and toned. His cock was as long as mine was, but thinner. Paul stripped, as we got naked. He was hairless and he shaved his pubes. You could have mistaken him for a boy of 12 or 13 were it not for his cock. He had an adult cock.

"I know I asked Paul if I could just see you," Thompson said. "Would you mind if I touched it?" he asked. He was staring at my cock like a deer caught in the headlights; he was transfixed.

"I'm not the shy type," I said. Both Thompson and Paul came over. One stroked my cock while the other fondled my balls. A cell phone rang. Thompson jumped and answered it. "I'll be there in fifteen minutes," he said. "I'm at the club." He hung up. "I have to go," he said. "Playtime is over." He quickly got dressed and left.

"Noland, you're one ugly man!" Paul said. "I can't believe you turned him on. I guess there's no accounting for taste."

"I guess you're right about that," I said.

"You do have one hell of a cock," he said as he buttoned up his shirt.

"So I've been told." I remarked as I went back to work. I wanted to find out if the session with Thompson was recorded. I wasn't sure how I'd do that. In the evening, I checked my room for cameras and microphones. I didn't find any. Room 8 was furnished with many mirrors and I assumed these concealed the cameras.

Johnson appeared at my room at 10:30 and Jack arrived a few minutes later. Both men were nervous as hell, but at least they made it. Lust overwhelmed caution once again. We made some casual chitchat. Jack and Johnson were alike in many ways. It was easy to see they were attracted to each other, but neither was bold enough to do anything about it.

I got the ball rolling. "I know you guys have just met, but I know you both. We're all members of the same club, and I don't mean the Mandrake Club. I'm ready to have some fun, and I'm hoping you men are ready too," I said.

"I'm not sure..." Johnson started to say.

"Boys, I am sure," I said. "You guys aren't going to win any awards for self awareness. I think you're so horny and hot-to-trot you're about ready to explode. Am I right?"

"You're right," Jack admitted.

Johnson nodded. I went on, "We're all adults. We all know what we want. You may not know how to get what you want, but I know and I can give you some lessons. It time to strip naked and get it on!" My little pep talk did the trick. Jack and Johnson were both well beyond half hard by the time they were nude. They both liked what they saw in the other.

There is an uncomfortable period between getting naked and starting sex. I did my bit to keep that period as short as possible, as in two or three seconds. Once mouths sucked cocks, all was well. I was pleased. We formed a small daisy chain on my bed, linked cock to mouth. We rotated a few times, so everyone sampled all the equipment.

It was exciting, but got more so when I got Jack and Johnson to 69. Both men were well equipped, but they could deep throat each other easily. My cock is more exciting as a novelty item, than it is suited for day-to-day use. It's like those huge dildos you see in Adult Novelty stores. It's a good conversation piece, and fun at parties, but too big for every day.

I could tell Jack and Johnson were made for each other. The sucking was good, but the fucking got even better. Since Johnson had fucked me, I suggested he screw Jack as prelude for me revisiting Jack's ass. Both men were game. Johnson came close to shooting when I suggested it.

It's not every day you get to see two men finding the meaning of life. They were both excited. Jack was on his back and Johnson got his leg on his shoulders. I lubricated both of them. Johnson positioned his cock at Jack's hole and pushed gingerly. It was a bit too gingerly.

"Push harder!" Jack ordered. Johnson did as he was told. His big cock head popped into Jack's ass. When it cleared the sphincter, both men sighed in satisfaction. The cock slid easily into the love tunnel. I could sense both men getting more excited as the cock went deeper. Sometimes you can tell when there's a perfect fit. This was one of these times.

Johnson was really close to shooting, but I got him to slow down. He made it a good ten minutes before he shot off. He was a pound lighter and Jack was a pound heavier after Johnson shot his load. When Johnson pulled out, I took his place.

Jack's semen lubricated ass welcomed my cock like an old friend. Jack was more than receptive. I was in the mood for a long fuck, and Jack was fine with that. We switched positions and I fucked him from the rear as Jack was on his side. By then Johnson had recovered from his orgasm. He cuddled up to Jack and they began to kiss.

The kiss turned into a full-fledged make out session. They were going at it hot and heavy. Jack was kissing Johnson as I fucked him. It was good for all of us. I shot off.

"You still have fully loaded balls?" I asked of Jack. He nodded.

"It's okay," he said. "This has been really good."

"I'd be glad to take care of you," I said. "My ass is available. You could scratch an itch I have about six inches in my ass. Maybe Johnson could help you too."

"I've never been fucked," Johnson said.

"Do you think you like to give it a spin?" I asked. He didn't answer, but I knew they both wanted it. "Jack can take his time," I said. Johnson was very excited, but nervous. I got him on his back. Jack and I shared lubricating duties on Johnson's ass. Johnson's ass wasn't particularly tight and his prostate was in working order.

Johnson didn't know what was going on. I don't think he knew he had a prostate. When I took my finger out, he returned to earth. As soon as Jack's cock touched Johnson's ass, it was love at first thrust. I have heard men talking about a hungry ass, but never experienced it until I saw Johnson's ass swallow Jack's cock.

Remarkably, Jack took his time and they had a nice long session. Jack shot off and Johnson had another ball busting orgasm. Two very happy men left my room that night. I had a good time playing Cupid.

A big thunderstorm that night woke me. I couldn't get to sleep again so I did a little exploring in the garden. Room 8 was empty and I got in the door to the back room easily. It had been a bad storm, so I did a little constructive electrical work. I connected a few wires and shorted the system out. I hoped it would be written off as a lightning strike.

Part 6

The blackmail machine was out of operation for a short while. I felt good about that, but there was more to do. I went into the club and found Carlton at the main desk.

"Where's the night watchman?" I asked.

"He didn't show up," Carlton said. "I get to pinch hit."

"Do you have a full house tonight?" I asked.

"All except for the guest room and DeBoer's room," Carlton said. "He's in New York for an early morning talk program."

"Have you ever been in his room?" I asked.

"Nope," he replied.

"Want to take a look?" I asked.

"How would you get in? I don't have a key"

"If you would like to stand shotgun, I might be able to get in the room," I said. "If worse comes to worse, you can catch me."

Carlton smiled at me. "Room 7," he said. We went up stairs to room 7. It was at the end of the hall and apart from the other rooms. It had a modern lock, but I had the manufacturer's master key. We had a retired locksmith working for Clydesdale & Company. I had learned a lot from him. The door opened easily after two or three minutes of fiddling. I opened the door slowly. There is always the chance someone was in the room.

The room was empty. The room was a plain old bedroom with nothing out of the ordinary. A door led to a second room. This apparently originally had been a small apartment for a servant. Computers and monitors filled this room. To one side was a big mass storage device. The computers were sleeping. I jiggled a mouse and one of the computers came to life.

I went to see if I could get a directory of the hard drives. Unbelievably, there was no password protection. DeBoer was very confident of the room's security. He had named the files by the date of the recording. I clicked on yesterday's date. A media player popped up and I was looking at one of the older members sucking Paul's cock. I pressed the skip button. I was watching Lonnie fucking another member. Carlton came in the room and saw the movie. "Oh shit!" he exclaimed. "That's his game. He's a voyeur."

I looked at him. I must not have had my poker face on.

"It's worse than that, isn't it?" Carlton whispered. I nodded. "What can we do?"

"There was a bad lightening strike nearby earlier. It could have done some damage," I said. I went to the bathroom, got a glass of water and poured some into the computer. It shorted out. We left the room. Carlton returned to the main desk.

It might not have stopped the recording, but it would take a while to fix things. That would give me some time. The next day was uneventful. DeBoer stayed in New York, so his computer problems were undiscovered. Carlton came to see me and said DeBoer had called. "He wanted to know if there was a problem with the phones," Carlton said. "I told him there had been a bad electrical storm and we had been some problems. I said my computer modem had burned out. I said modems were very susceptible to electric surges."

"You done well," I said.

"Do I get a reward for being good?" he asked.

"You sure do, but not here," I said. "I'll drop by your apartment." Carlton left. That evening I went on a walk. This was my best chance to make a cell call to my office. I had gone a block when I noticed a car was following me. I went into a shop, got a coke and started to walk back to the Club. The car was waiting. The car window rolled down.

"Taking the evening air?" a voice asked. It was Thompson.

"The club gets stuffy," I said.

"I live a few blocks away, would you like to join me for a drink?" he asked. I said, "Okay," and joined him in the car. Thompson's idea of a few blocks wasn't mine. We were in Alexandria when he pulled into a garage under a high-rise condominium tower. We went up to the top floor. Thompson had a penthouse apartment.

"I take it your wife is away?" I asked. He looked shocked. You could tell a woman lived in the apartment, but he obviously didn't know it was that obvious. "Don't worry; I'm not a kiss and tell kind of guy. I like fun. I'm not looking to get married."

"I'm terrified of being outed," he said. "It would ruin me."

"As I said, I'm not looking to get married. Your life is your life, it's none of my business," I said. "I was hoping we'd get naked and finish what we started the other day."

"I'm not a very adventurous man," Thompson said. "I guess they call it plain vanilla."

"There's nothing wrong with plain vanilla, as long as there's enough of it," I said. He smiled. We went to the bedroom. Thompson was taking his shirt off as we walked. He was ready.

Thompson was hard and ready to suck by the time we got to his bedroom. He was not a novice, and he came close to deep throating me. We got on his bed and 69ed. He was hung long rather than thick and had a good pair of balls. He was enthusiastic when he was sucking, but seemed disinterested when he wasn't connected to my cock.

He was a heavy leaker. While he pretended to be cool and detached, his cock and balls were fully involved. They weren't playing it cool at all. We were chatting during a break, when I got interested in his cock. Thompson's slender cock stood straight up. Covered with my spit, I decided to sit on it.

I caught him by surprise, but it was a pleasant surprise. It was a good fit for me. I leaned forward and played with Thompson's tits. I immediately felt him relax. As the tension drained from him, his cock twitched. I had found his on button.

Once I discovered his tits, I had him under my control. If he had a choice, Thompson would have stayed cool, but I didn't give him that chance. Thompson lost his dignity and his macho image, but he learned a lot about his own sexuality. He also discovered what sex is like when you give up on attitude and go with the flow.

He was a natural top, and soon I was on my back as he pounded me. At first, he was a pile driver, but when I played with his tits, he took his time. Pulling out just before he shot, Thompson gave me a sperm bath after fifteen or twenty minutes if high quality ass time. We took a shower to clean up and then returned to the bed. He was still hard, so I did a pole dance on his cock again and he went to the moon and back. He shot off big time in my ass. He had a nice, slow landing and we talked.

"Do you bottom?" I asked.

"Shit, I've never fucked a guy before," he admitted.

"It seems to me you are handling the new experience well," I said. I found out he was one of those men who loved his wife, but liked sex with men. There were pictures of her, with his children all over the bedroom. They were a handsome family. As he got older, his taste for men increased. From the way he talked, he was unprepared to deal with his passion for men, except for deep feeling of guilt and depression.

He also possessed a strong sex drive. He wanted sex with men, but was embarrassed and afraid if his desires. He was between a rock and a hard cock. During the course of the conversation I found out he was a lobbyist for a large defense contractor.

"Have you been a member of the Mandrake Club for long?" I asked.

"I'm not a member," he said. "As a matter of fact, some of my rival lobbyists are members. I always thought they were cut throat competitors, but they've been nice to me at the club."

"Are the waiters part of the club's membership services?" I asked.

"I'm not sure," Thompson said. "Martin, the guy who had been with me at the club, was really interested in having me meet Paul. Paul wasn't my cup-of-tea. I wouldn't normally do it, but Martin caught me at a horny time. Helen had just gone on European trip with our youngest daughter."

"Paul wasn't your cup of tea, but I am?" I asked.

"To tell you the truth, I didn't expect that," Thompson said. "Martin said you were well hung and I was curious. He said you weren't much to look at, but his friends said you were hung like a fucking horse. You're more than I expected."

"Handsome and dashing?"

He smiled. "No one would mistake you for a girl," he said. "You're all man."

"You like masculine men?"

"It seems that way to me," he said. "Unfortunately, I'm not a good judge of who is, or is not gay. I wouldn't have picked you out in a million years. Can you tell?"

"Not always, but when I'm naked I usually find out fast," I said. "Often Gay and straight men are both interested."

"Odd, isn't it?"

"I think being interested in cock is natural. I'll bet there was a lot of interest in cocks when we were naked cavemen on a hunting trip," I remarked. "On a long, dark and cold night your pal's cock would be both interesting and fun."

Thompson laughed. "You're an anthropologist? That seems like a stretch to me."

"Let's face it. All men have the same equipment and most of us are oversexed. Our sex organs are in easy reach and ain't it nice our prostates are within a cock's length up our ass." I said. "Women are moody. As far as I can tell, men are ready 24-7."

Thompson sucked me for a while and I shot off. He liked watching the jiz spurt, and the post orgasmic drool from my slit. My orgasm wasn't as spectacular as his was, but my cock looked like it had been sugar glazed when it was over. As the ejaculations diminished, he got close and stuck his tongue out to intercept the sperm.

He took my entire cock head into his mouth and pushed his tongue into the slit to get the sperm when it was still steamy and fresh from my balls. He was hard as a rock again. He had a third visit to my ass.

I took the Metro back to the club. It gave me a chance to call my office and my client. I summarized my suspicions for Mr. Willamette. The Mandrake Club was a center for right wing activity. The membership had a high percentage of military officers, defense industry executives, lobbyists and fellow travelers. Only a few knew the sexual aspect of to club membership. You had to be a real insider to know that.

Curiously, the military men were mostly of the armchair and theoretical sort, or involved in procurement. I could smell money. As far as I could tell, all of the members were conservative, so the blackmail wasn't intended to embarrass or humiliate them. They were all on the same side.

"My son was working on advance stealth technology for the navy," Willamette said, "That fits your profile. Was the blackmail intended to direct contracts to specific companies?"

"That would be my guess," I said. "One more thing, there is no evidence that poor judgment, incompetence and outright steeling are an impediment to job advancement in the armed forces. Homosexuality is a career ender."

"My son wouldn't play ball?" he asked.

"That too is my guess, but it's also possible he found out about the recording system. Maybe he told someone," I suggested. "He may have trusted the wrong person. Do you know any of his friends?"

"Why? Do you think they betrayed him?"

"No, I was wondering about his taste in men," I answered. "The staff here is weighted toward young looking men. In a blackmail situation, sex with a boy would be more damning."

"I really don't know. He was an athlete in school. He wasn't good enough to play varsity in college, but he was good in prep school, Mr. Willamette said. "Most of the friends I met tended to be jocks."

I got back to the club at 11:30 and actually got a full night's sleep. No one dropped by. DeBoer returned and discovered the damaged equipment. Carlton reported to me that he was out of sorts and fuming. I was interested in seeing who would come to fix them.

I was in the garden and saw men from the Capital Computer Company go into the room at the rear of Room 8. About ten minutes later DeBoer and his friend came out. DeBoer looked as if he was fit to be tied.

"How long will it take to fix this fucking thing?" he screamed. I couldn't hear the response, but DeBoer yelled, "A week! You've got to be kidding! I need it fixed in two days!" I couldn't hear the rest. DeBoer sounded like a three year old trying to get his way. Unlike the child, he possessed ready cash. He must have calmed down. "I don't care about the cost. Have it fixed in 48 hours," DeBoer said, closing the conversation with the worker.

Servants tend to disappear into the background. I all but vanish. I was born to be innocuous. That day I was working on leveling up a brick path, so I was on my knees. The men from the computer company walked around me as they went about their work, but didn't pay any attention. One of the men cell phoned his boss and explained the situation. They didn't know what had happened but didn't suspect sabotage.

"I have no idea what happened out here in the carriage house," he said. "Inside it's the fat guy's fault. He eats and drinks at the computer. He must have spilled something into it. He needs it done in two days. Cost is no object." The man on the other end said, "Thank you Jesus for rich assholes," so loud I could hear it eight feet away.

I saw Carlton and asked if anyone special was coming in a day or two. "Can't talk now," he said. "I talk to you later."

That afternoon, the garden was a hive of activity as the computer people rushed to fix the system. One of the computer technicians was a heavy-set, bearded man. He had the body of like a forty year old, but I soon realized he was in his twenties. He was the low man on the totem pole did most of the heavy lifting. He noticed me.

The day turned warm, and my brickwork was hard. He looked at my hairy chest and me. I had unbuttoned my shirt. "Damn you're a hairy guy," he said. He was drinking a Coke as he took a break.

"I'm hairy everywhere but on my eyes and tongue," I said.

He laughed. "Most girls hate hairy men," he said.

"To tell you the truth, I'm not much into girls," I said.

He looked at me and winked. "I guess you could say that about me," he whispered. I smiled back. "I'll be here most of the night," he said. "My name's Luther."

"I have a room in the basement. I'm Noland," I said. He went back to work. At five, I cleaned up the sidewalk area and went to my room. I think Luther was watching. He knocked on my door minute after I got in my room. When I opened the door, he looked confused. I was shirtless by then. I guessed he had gotten up enough nerve to knock on the door, but hadn't figured out what to do next.

"Come on in," I said. Luther looked relieved and came in. He was wearing a shirt with a company logo. It was partially unbuttoned, showing off a thick pelt of curly, dirty blond hair.

"Damn you're hairy," he said in what was almost a moan.

"I take it you like that?"

"Big time," he said. "Do you think maybe I could drop by later tonight?" he asked. "Maybe we could get to know each other better?"

"I'm not much into social calls," I said. He looked crest fallen. "That is unless some hot sex is involved." Luther looked as if he had received and electric shock. Then he smiled.

"Let me be straight with you," I said. "I'm an older guy who likes to run things. I've got lots of friends and don't need more. I'm not looking for an LTR, or planning to get married in Canada. I do like long, hot and sweaty sex, no holds barred. I like it to last and get off."

"Do I get to get off too?" Luther whispered.

I laughed, "I can guarantee it," I said. "How long does it take for you to recharge after you've popped your nut?"

"It takes fifteen, maybe twenty minutes."

"How many times can you shoot off in a night?"

"Four, maybe five times," Luther said. "That's jerking off. I'm never done it that many times with another guy."

"This may be your lucky day," I said. He had to get back to work. I told him I would be in my room after ten. Luther nodded and left. It was five o'clock now. He was going to have the longest five hours of his life.

Ten minutes later, there was another knock at my door. I guessed Luther had lost his nerve, but it was Carlton. "I've only got a half hour," he said. I was wearing only my jockeys by then. He stripped at light speed and sucked me until I was hard. He was on his back with my cock tenderizing his ass in five minutes.

I asked him if there were any special guests coming to the club in two days. "Is room 8 booked?"

"There's a big shindig coming up. The manager is handling it personally," Carlton said. "There is a luncheon at 12:00 for ten. The conference room is booked too, as is room 8."

"Who's serving the lunch?" I asked. I was doing slow, deep strokes so Carlton could think.

"Lon, Paul and Henry are signed up," Carlton said. "Henry's a new guy. You'd swear he was 14, but he's 25 and a piece of work. I thought I like taking it in the ass, but he's a professional, 100% bottom, pig slut."

"What is the group?"

"That I don't know, but no pork is to be served," Carlton said. "Lewis says it not a kosher lunch, so it probably some brand of Arab. DeBoer and his pal Hatfield are running the show." I picked up my pace and Carlton had a more than satisfactory orgasm. He returned to work. I went out for dinner and got back by 9:00. The computer geeks were still at work in the garden. It was just Luther and another man. It was a pleasant night, so I sat in a corner of the garden.

At 9:30, Luther's sidekick left. I heard Luther saying, "I'll take care of the rest of this. You get home to Donna." The other man left quickly. I returned to my room. Luther appeared at 10:00 on the dot. I gave him a beer to relax. "Is there any way I can take a shower?" he asked. It was too early for the club locker room, but my bathroom had an undersized tub in with a hand shower. He went to the bathroom and I heard the water going. It was show and tell time, so I joined him.

Luther was a pleasant surprise. He looked as if he still had his baby fat, but his heavy lifting must have turned most of it into muscle. He was solid. Luther was hairy front, back and middle. I got in the tub. There was barely room for his massive body. I solved that problem by getting on my knees and sucking him. At first, he was all balls and head. All three were apricot sized. He had a cut cock and the flared head covered whatever shaft there was. The slit was a good half-inch wide and he spurted something sweet and sticky the second my tongue touched it.

I was pretty happy with what I found, but it got better. Luther possessed a perfect example of what I called a telescoping cock. As I sucked him, it emerged inch by inch until he had a solid seven inches of rock hard man meat. He jumped when I first touched his asshole, but the next time he was okay with it.

"Let's get out of here," I said. "We need to spread out some." We dried off and went to the bedroom. Luther sat on the bed when he got his first good view of my cock. The tub and bath were so tight it was hard to see.

"Jesus Christ, what in hell have I got myself into?" he exclaimed.

I laughed. "I take it you don't bottom much?" I asked.

"I've done it a few times, but never with anything like yours."

"I never shove it where it won't fit," I said. "You've got a nice wide mouth." He took the hint. Luther had no problem with my cock. He was a big man and he was able to deep throat me after a few tries. He was at the upper limit of what I could deep throat, but I did it too. We both deep throated together and Luther shot off. His balls made a rich and creamy brew and it was good.

His recharge time was 12 minutes. Luther returned to sucking me.

Part 7

Luther sucked me until I shot off. I warned him I was going to blow, but he didn't mind. He sucked until I was dry.

"You're good at that," I said.

Luther came up for air. "That was good," he said. "I've never taken the jiz before. It wasn't what I thought."

"Are you new to this?"

"I'm not exactly new to it, but I'm not that experienced either," he said. He chuckled. "Actually I haven't done it in a bed."

"You're waiting for the State Trooper to walk into the rest stop rest room?"

"How did you know that?" he asked.

"We've all been there," I said. "Relax. We've got some time."

Luther wasn't experienced, but he wasn't shy at all. My cock transfixed him and he was either looking at it, or playing with it as we talked. I asked him about his job. "We do specialty audio and video recording," he said, "real top dollar stuff. If you want it yesterday and are made of money, we're your guys."

"I didn't know the club had that much money," I said.

"They aren't paying for it. The fat guy is," Luther said. "He has some sort a deal with the boss. He does a lot of this sort of things. We've installed a few other set ups."

"In the club?"

"No. One was in a hotel suite and another in a private club," he answered.

"More private than the Mandrake club?"

Luther laughed. "It was a whore house, The DuPont Modeling Agency," he said. "It is a very upscale fancy house with a lot of pretty women. They didn't look like hookers, but that's what they were. I figured given the way DeBoer looks, he needs to pay for it."

"And he wants a souvenir?"

"I guess so. We just install the systems," he explained. "We never see the product."

"It seems kind of odd to me." I said.

"When you get paid as much as we do, we don't ask questions," Luther said. "The boss told me if I asked a question I'd be fired. That's the rule. I shouldn't have told you about it."

I started sucking him again. He took the hint. There was no more shoptalk. There was some sex talk.

"Are you into fucking?" he asked.

"I am."

"Do you top? Bottom?" Luther asked.

"I do both," I replied, "What about you?"

"I've never really done it," he said. "A guy tried once but he just fucked my cheeks. He didn't get into my ass. I think I'd like it."

"Which would you prefer top or bottom?"

"I would mind trying to do both," Luther replied, "but I have a feeling you're not the guy to be a teacher. I was thinking of a more modest cock for my maiden voyage."

"Actually I'm a good teacher, but my cock isn't for just anyone," I said. "You have to really want it."

"I want it," Luther whispered. "Really bad."

I licked a finger and began working it into his ass. "Let's just see how far I can go," I said. Luther jumped a little when I first touched his asshole, but he relaxed immediately and let me in. After a minute or two of probing, I found Luther's prostate; he was primed and ready. It was plump and supple.

I had noticed Luther was a good sport. While he wasn't experienced, he was more than receptive and a fast learner. When I pressed his prostate, he moaned. I got two fingers in and pressed it from each side. He shivered and shook in pleasure.

"What was that?" Luther asked.

"That little organ is going to make this into a really good evening for you," I said as I pressed it again. Luther moaned. His ass lost any ability to resist. Luther was open. He also wasn't particularly tight. I worked a third finger into his pliable ass. There was no effort to keep it out.

"Do you think you could take something bigger in your ass?" I asked.

"You're awfully big," he said. He was silent for a few seconds, and then he whispered, "I'd like to try."

"Do you trust me to be careful?" I asked, "It's easier if you're relaxed."

"As long as it doesn't hurt," Luther said.

"I can't promise that. Sometimes it doesn't fit exactly right on the first try," I explained. "You tell me if it's too much." Luther nodded. I had some lube and poppers available. Luther knew about poppers and looked relieved when he saw I had them.

I got him on his back with his legs on my shoulders. I lubricated him when I finger fucked his hole, but I coated my meat. I pushed my knob gently into his hole. I just bounced it and felt his sphincter giving way. I bounced a few more times and he opened up. It was almost as if his ass was swallowing my cock.

My cock head slid in and the shaft was right behind it. Luther tensed, but as I pushed deeper he relaxed. His balls were resting on my bush and my entire cock was deep in his ass. Luther was moaning and whimpering a little, but he remained rock hard. He hadn't needed the poppers.

I began to make several short thrusts. With each thrust, pre cum oozed from Luther's cock. My cock was perfectly at home in Luther's rectum. Luther couldn't get enough of it, so we just screwed for the next hour or so. We tried a few snorts of amyl and got really crazy. We calmed down to easy fucking. By then he was wearing out, so I sat on his cock. It was a good fit too. His cock head was just the right length to massage my prostate. I balanced on it and as I undulated my ass on his love pole, I got carried away. It was good for both of us. Luther left at midnight. I wouldn't have guessed Luther could take my cock on his maiden voyage, but he must have been a natural bottom. It couldn't have been any better for him, or for me.

That night I dreamed of Mr. DeBoer. He was a busy man. If Luther was right, he was covering the gay angle at the club and the heterosexual side at the whorehouse. I needed my office to dig deeper into his activities. I knew nothing about DeBoer's sidekick, Hatfield and still didn't have any information on the All America foundation.

In my dream, I was fucking the admiral, but he was trying to get one of the women to come over so he could screw her. I was miffed he was switch-hitting. "My cock's more than enough," I complained. I didn't have a restful night.

Luther was back the next morning and they worked like dogs and got the system up and running again. I had hoped it would take more time. There would be the event the next day, and that might give me an opportunity to see the operation in action.

While I was sweeping the walk, Johnson stopped by to talk. "You sure have the place looking good," he said. "You've been busy."

"My Momma said I might not look like much, but I wasn't lazy," I said.

Johnson leaned nearer. "Are you going to be free tonight?" he asked.

"As far as I know," I replied. "Sometimes guys just drop by, but they're guys you'd like." He understood what I was saying and continued on his way. DeBoer left in a hurry after talking to Luther's boss. He looked aggravated. I think aggravated was his normal condition. I was back working on the walk and overheard Luther talking with his boss.

"We break our asses getting this job done and he's still pissed," Luther said.

"Welcome to the real world," the boss said. "I've never gotten a thank you or good job from him. He'll complain about the bill too."

"Will he pay it?" Luther asked.

"He sure as shit will," the boss replied. "If anyone found out what he was doing his fat ass would be toast."

"I don't think I'd like that toast," Luther said.

His boss laughed. "I don't know exactly what he's up to, but I could find out real easily. The fat guy knows it and he will pay." A few days later, Luther's boss was dead. He was killed in a hit and run accident. I wasn't fooled for a minute.

Johnson wasn't able to make it that night, so I had a chance to rest and get in touch with my office. Technically the All America Foundation was a well-respected academic organization with distinguished members paid for by public-spirited multimillionaires. Behind them were large, multinational corporations engaged in defense and intelligence operations. These weren't the big names I was familiar with, but more obscure corporations.

On my early morning walk, I just happened to run into Red. He was in a van two blocks from the Club. I was being watched. He gave me a quick rundown on the situation. He was investigating an outbreak of defective equipment and intelligence. Some of the new weaponry failed to operate properly. The United States had insisted on these, in spite of questions about the reliability of the weapons. Potentially more serious was the out-sourcing of intelligence.

American intelligence wasn't matching NATO or British information. As the 800-pound Gorilla in the room, the United States carried the day. Red was to find out why the U.S. was so insistent on the false information.

"You think it blackmail that gives the false info its allure?" I asked.

"I think that is part of it," Red said. "Admittedly there are some who simply have a warped sense of reality. Those we discount automatically."

"Would this group include a Mr. DeBoer or perhaps a Mr. Hatfield?" I asked.

"You' are brighter than you look," Red replied. "Our problem was with normally levelheaded men who were pushing the bad info strongly. We were puzzled until Commander Willamette came forward. He told his British counterpart about the blackmail in outline form. Before he had a chance to fill out the details and name names, he was floating in the reflecting basin."

"We don't know how the men are seduced," he said. "Do you have some thoughts?"

"The men I've met are closeted gay, very conventional men. They move in conservative circles and I think genuinely believe in the family value shit," I said. "They are stunningly unaware of their true sexual orientation and living in fear they will be caught. It's as if they are living in the 1950s. They also are ambitious and driven."

"Easy marks?"

"Terrified of discovery," I said. "As far as I can tell, they are a blackmailer's dream. The cameras are set up at the club and at a whorehouse somewhere."

"That must be Cathedral Manor," Red said, "It's a small apartment house near the National Cathedral."

"I thought it was the DuPont Modeling Agency," I said.

"They are one and the same. The agency's digs are in the Cathedral Manor Apartments," Red said, "Congressman Deutch has an apartment there."

"I don't know of him."

"He's ultra Catholic, well to the right of the Pope and much holier than Mother Theresa. On the floor below is Ellenna DuPont. She's is the upscale madam," Red explained.

"She's a DuPont?"

Red smiled. "That's her nom-de-cunt. She's was born as Helena DiPaulo in Johnstown, PA. She looks good and has a stable of helpers. Deutch had a warm spot for hookers. He seems to think some pure Catholic sperm shot up their pussy will save them."

"My kind of guy," I said.

"The working girls hate him, but he shoots off fast and pays very well," Red said. "They are paid by the hour."

"Do they know their being photographed?" I asked.

"The marks don't," Red said. "My sources say the ladies get paid extra if photographs are involved."

"Do you know their clients?"

"No, but we will soon enough," Red said.

"I need to get back to work," I said. I got back

Officially, the club was closed for DeBoer's special event. Only residents and staff were allowed in the building. The club was filled with activity, as the kitchen and housekeeping staffs got ready for meeting. I was pressed into service to do valet parking. The men all arrived in big

Mercedes or SUV's. Not one of these was designed for the club's tight parking lot. I had a chance to see most of the men and talk with their drivers. The visitors were mostly American businessmen, but there were several Arabs in business dress and a few Europeans.

I got along well with one of the Arab's driver, an Indian name Ravi. He had been in the country a while and seemed to think I was a Hillbilly. I tried to explain I wasn't a hillbilly; I was just a country boy from south-west Virginia. He was unconvinced. "My customer will like you," he said.

I tried to keep an eye on Room 8. Periodically a guest of two would wonder out to the room. They would knock and someone would let them in. An hour or so later the guests would leave to make room for another one of the visitors. One or two would stay for fifteen or twenty minutes only.

Around 3:00, Ravi came to me and asked if I would meet his customer, "The man has never met a Hillbilly before," he said.

"I'm supposed to be working."

"Don't worry about that, the manager said it's all right," Ravi whispered. "He said you're a friendly man too. He said you might take a shower to clean up before meeting Abdul." I agreed, went to my room and then took a shower.

A tall, thin, well-dressed, bearded man entered the locker room and looked in the shower. He just stared. I turned off the shower and dried off, then joined him in the locker room. He didn't seem to have a plan. "My bedroom is next door," I said. I wrapped a towel around my waist and left. He followed.

Once we were in a private space, he relaxed. "Are you named Jethro?" he asked.

I smiled. "Noland's the name, but I know a lot of Bubbas, Skeeters and Scooters."

"Abdul here," he said as he reached over and fondled my cock. "You are a stallion." He had an English accent.

"I'm a short stallion," I said. "Why don't we get naked and have some fun?" Abdul was ready. He stripped quickly and tried to swallow my cock in one gulp. He got about half, but he liked what he got.

He was much younger than I had thought, maybe 25, and had a hairy chest linked to his bush by a treasure trail. I only got a glimpse of his cock, but it looked fine, long and cut.

"Are you a Beverly Hillbillies' fan?" I asked, "Or is it the Dukes of Hazard?"

He looked up at me and smiled. "The Dukes," he said. "I loved them as a kid. You look like the guys at the gas station."

"I've done my stint in gas stations," I said. "You were educated in England?"

"Yes, but this is my first trip to the United States," Abdul said. "This is the first time my bodyguards let me get close to a man of your..."

"Rank?" I suggested.

"That will do," he said. "I have never been with a man like you. You are so odd looking." he looked at me with a worried look in his eyes. "Have I insulted you?"

"Hell no," I answered. "I'm not sure rank or looks has anything to do with cocks. The distribution of cock seems to be unrelated to wealth, or position. God has a sense of humor."

"I'm not very experienced in these things. Is your cock as big as I think it is?" he asked.

"That's what they tell me. I've met a few who were bigger, but not that many." I said as I maneuvered him to the bed. I began to suck him. His meat was long, thin and curved, with a bloated cock head. It was just right for sucking. He came close to shooting when my tongue touched his head. He moaned.

"Calm down. We have time. You've got a hair trigger."

"This is wonderful," he moaned.

Part 8

Abdul was 24 years old, but this was his first time out of the sight of his bodyguards and servants. He was educated at Oxford, but had been in a protective cocoon. His father was a government official for a Gulf state who had suffered a heart attack. The King delegated Abdul to fill in for him. It was apparently a hereditary position. While he didn't say it, he was clearly a Prince of some sort and filthy rich.

He had some sexual experience with his schoolmates, but he had never been with an adult male. Abdul liked it. He wanted sex with a real man, not another boy. He had never been to the United States and had hopes the US would be a hillbilly, or cowboy fantasy. I was as close as he could come in Washington, D.C.

I think he would have been disappointed if it hadn't been for my cock. He was use to pretty, English boys and boy cocks. My cock is big, uncut and oozing. It's not at all pretty. He liked my deep voice, southern accent and hairy body. I'm a home grown, all-American red neck, and Abdul thought I was exotic and exciting.

I have to admit I'm not that use to having sex with a handsome Arab prince, but I sure can go with the flow. In some ways, he was like Luther, inexperienced, but eager. He wanted intense and exciting sex, but didn't know what it would actually be like. He was willing to experiment.

I wasn't sure how far he would go and was a bit uneasy about doing it with a prince. It might be a shock.

Abdul was nervous. "Are you rough?" he asked.

"Nope, I just look that way," I said. "I like sex to be good for me and good for my playmate. I can't enjoy it if my partner doesn't have fun."

"Are most men like that?" he asked.

"The men I know are," I replied. "Some guys are into power, or proving something. I'm not into that. I'm not into sadomasochism at all. Why mix pain with pleasure?"

"That makes sense to me," Abdul said. "I don't know the rules. I've seen some movies. Sometimes the men aren't nice. I didn't know if that was part of sex."

"It's not for me," I said. "Man sex can be messy. It's good when cum and precum are all over the place. Sex isn't good if you're a neat freak. What are you interested in?"

Rather than answer me, he returned to sucking my cock. I eventually discovered Abdul was more experienced than I thought, just not with pre-adult males. His ass wasn't virgin and he had enjoyed several well-endowed friends.

Abdul had no experience with grown men, hairy men, or working class men. All three turned him on big time. I had no idea what happened to a man when three of his sexual obsessions occur in the same person, but I found out. Abdul turned in to a six-foot tall erogenous zone. Every time my furry body touched his, it was acutely pleasurable for him.

We sucked, sixty-nined and then he guided my cock into his quivering ass. He loved it and took his time savoring it as each inch slipped into his body. Most of the time I notice a man's hot spots, but Abdul's asshole, sphincter and rectum were all tender and responsive. He shot off when I had five inches in him and again when the entire organ was embedded. He collapsed in exhaustion after the second orgasm. I held him as he recharged.

My cock popped out of his ass, so I turned is over and entered from the rear. He loved it when I pumped my cock and rubbed my chest hair against his back. I'm not a particularly cuddly man, but I think Abdul was use to the slam-bang-thank-you-ma'am school of sex. My approach alternating a slow build-up with wild climaxes was good. He liked the body contact too.

He fucked me next. Abdul was a pile driver. I got him to slow down and smell the roses. He was easily coverted to my approach. He seemed to have been with boys who were single mindedly directed towards the orgasm. While I like ball draining ejaculations as much as any guy, I also like quality cock-time. Fifteen minutes of cock stimulation before an orgasm is a lot better than five.

We were together an hour and a half before he had to go back to the meeting. Abdul was discrete about the meeting, but it seemed to be a low-key sales effort for weapons and software. They could afford to be low key if the actual purpose of the meeting was to get the potential buyers into embarrassing situations for future blackmail. I wondered if the blackmail involved showing favoritism for a particular product rather than cash. That would be hard to trace or prove.

If it worked that way, it would also be particularly financially rewarding. You usually measure blackmail in thousands of dollars, but given the price of weapons, the return would be in the millions. Stories about failed multimillion-dollar software systems, or weapons scrapped after years of development fill newspapers. Ten or twenty million could vanish in the blink of an eye and no one would be the wiser.

I went on a walk after dinner and Red appeared. I must have been under surveillance every time I left the Club. I was four, or five blocks from the club when he appeared on the side walk ahead of me. He turned into an apartment house and I followed him. He went into an apartment and left the door open.

When I entered he asked, "I was wondering how long it would take for you to notice I was with you?"

"How long was it?"

"Less than a minute," Red said. "You're good at this. Is there any news to report?" I told him about my interlude with Abdul.

"Prince Abdul is one of the rising stars. He is tapped to be the defense minister when his father dies," Red said. "He's pro western and rational, as far as we can tell. He might become the next King, and his pro western and progressive tendencies could be a blessing for us." I explained my theory about the blackmail scheme.

"It seemed to be conventional blackmail at the beginning, but something was off," Red said. "Most of the men are well off, but not wealthy. It seems they might start with cash and then switch to getting them to give false recommendations when the men get financially desperate. Most of them think they are just shaving the truth a little bit. Commander Willamette had a strong technical background. He could tell when the system he was asked to push was shit."

"What's the story about the All America Group?" I asked.

"Technically it's a conservative think tank," Red said. "Its members have string relationships with defense contractors. DeBoer is getting "finder's fees." His sidekick, Hatfield is secretly on the board of the Enterprise Group. The Enterprise Group consists of a cluster of fly by night "consulting" firms. Most of these have a few retired army officers on the staff with some former staffers from Capitol Hill. Until three or four years ago, they got leftovers, projects too small for the big boys to do. They began getting bigger contracts from Homeland Security and Defense in the post 9/11 panic."

"As long as you are patriotic you might as well make a profit?" I suggested.

"A profit is all well and good, but they have moved into the fraud level," Red said. "They are basically anti government types. They don't have a problem cheating it. The budgets are huge, mostly unaccounted for and much is wasted in fraud and inefficiency. You have men fighting a war in a desert with poor weapons and intelligence, while the consultants sitting in plush offices are raking it in. It's a nasty business."

"What happens next?" I asked.

"Maybe you could mention to some of your pals you found recording devices in one of the rooms," Red said. "That might mix things up some. It would be interesting to see what happens." I left the apartment went to the coffee shop where I had the run in with the panhandler earlier. It was crowded. I was finishing a Mocha Java God knows what when Jack came in. We chatted for a while and went out. "Jack, while I was working in the garden at the club I found something odd," I whispered. "There is a video recording system in one of the rooms."

Jack looked shocked. "Which room?" he asked.

"The room in the garden, Room 8."

"Oh shit!" he exclaimed. "How did you find out? Who's doing it?"

"One of the repair guys told me about it," I said. "You know we had an electric problem last week. Mr. DeBoer seemed to be giving directions to the electricians."

"Thanks for the info," Jack said as he left hurriedly. When I got back to the club, a man was waiting for me outside the rear entrance.

"Are you Noland?" he asked in an English accent. "Clydesdale No-land?"

"That's me."

"What's going on with Abdul?" he asked in a tone that could be interpreted as menacing.

"Who am I talking to?"

There was a pause. "I'm Ali, his bodyguard."

"Let's go inside and talk," I said. "I need to tell you something." I unlocked the door and we went to my room. Ali was big, and had a fierce looking face, mostly covered with an ink black beard.

"Who are you working for?" he asked. "The British?"

"I'm working for a private client," I said. "His interests and the British interests seem to coincide. There is some sort of a blackmail scheme going on here. One of the rooms is fitted with cameras."

"Is Abdul in danger?" Ali asked, "He told me about you."

"Not to my knowledge," I said. "Certainly not from me. This room isn't under surveillance."

"How do you know?"

"I gave the place a good going over," I said. "Looking for bugs is my business. One of the camera installers was here. He wasn't at all concerned. I think he'd have been uneasy if there was a camera."

"Is the America First Foundation involved?" Ali said. "The head of security thinks something smells with that group."

"I don't know if it's the foundation, or just the members who have the problem," I said. "It could be a front, or it could be an unwitting accomplice."

"They are rude, rather stupid men, I think," Ali remarked. "They think they know it all, but they know nothing. They are like bulls in a china shop. We couldn't figure out why they were doing so well. It didn't make any sense. They produce inferior products, but got some choice contracts."

"Are you Abdul's friend or a hired hand?"

"I'm his cousin. We are family," Ali replied. "We are very close."

"I don't think he has a problem," I said, "Others caught in the web do. The men behind the scheme seem to have a knack for finding men who are susceptible to blackmail. The victims are conservative men who haven't come to grips with their sexual preferences."

"Being exposed as gay would be an embarrassment for many men, but for these it would be the kiss of death. DeBoer and his pals have them trapped. I don't know how to get out of it. It's a crooked scheme, but exposing it would destroy their victims. The boys they use are all adults, but in a photo they could all pass for teenagers."

"Blackmail is that way," Ali observed.

"These boys play hard ball too," I said. "It's probable a naval officer, Commander William Willamette, was murdered to keep him quiet. I suspect he was going to expose the scheme. I have no idea who the actual hit man was."

"Let me assure you, no one plays harder ball that we do. I need to get back to Abdul," Ali said. "If I find out who the killer of your Commander friend, I will let you know." He glanced down at my crotch. "I wish I had more time." Ali left.

I figured I had stirred up the water enough for one day and went to bed. Johnson was in the excise room the next morning. I told him about the cameras. He looked like someone had sucker punched him.

"You're kidding?"

"Nope, that's what the guy told me," I said. "There are cameras in room 8. He didn't mention any other rooms."

"Are there any in your room?"

"No, I checked," I said. "There is another set up at an upscale cat house near the Cathedral. "How did you end up getting a room here?"

"Senator Thornhill suggested it," Johnson replied. "I was just elected and was lost here in the big city. He said it was economical and convenient. Do you think he knows about it?"

Thornhill was archconservative and an unreformed racist. He was a noted womanizer and fit the profile of the men involved in the scheme. I wondered if he visited Mrs. Dupont. "I have no idea if the Senator knows. The whole place seems strange to me."

"It's beginning to seem strange to me," Johnson said. "Everyone was so friendly here. Maybe they are too friendly. I got an odd feeling about the waiters once or twice."

"Were they making a pass at you?"

"To tell you the truth, they may have been doing that, but I was too dense to know what was up," Johnson explained. He looked me in the eye. "Am I in trouble?" He was almost crying. "Are you going to expose me? It would ruin me."

"Not in a million years," I said. "There may be something going on here, but I'm not part of it."

"I have to get to the Capitol. Is there anywhere we can meet away from here?" Johnson asked.

"Let me think about that," I said. "Drop by this evening, if you can."

Part 9

Sometime during the next day, the shit hit the fan. I later found out Johnson went to see Senator Thornhill. The distinguished senator resigned from the Senate late that afternoon. He was going home to spend more time with his family. DeBoer and Hatfield were to be in Washington for a week, but had a sudden change of plans and went out of town. At ten that evening, Luther appeared with several other men to take out the recording system.

I noticed a car outside the club and saw an Arab in one of them. As I walked by, he got out and followed me. I went around the corner. There I ran into Red. The three of us had little conference.

"This is Ali, he's part of Prince Abdul's security. They're clearing out of the club?" Red asked. He didn't know I knew Ali.

"It looks like that to me," I said.

"We can't let them take the video recordings. I want them," Red said.

"I agree," Ali said. "I want to get them."

"What if the recordings were destroyed?" I asked. "It might be better if no one got the recordings. I think you are nice guys, but it would be better for everyone if there was no temptation."

"You might lose the evidence to need to find Commander Willamette's murderer," Red said.

"I'm afraid too many men would be ruined by these recordings," I said. "I think I'll take the risk."

"How do we get them?" Ali asked.

"The computer technician taking the system out is a pal of mine," I said. "I might be able to work something out."

"There may be a more direct way," Ali said. "I have some security contractors who could help out."

"I'm thinking the less fuss the better," I said. "If my tech friend can help, there will be no finger prints on anything." Ali looked me in the eye, and then agreed. "Are there other copies of the recordings?"

"Good news on that front," Red said. "We've intercepted the DSL connection for DeBoer's room. He's not sending things out from the room. As far as we can tell information goes into the room, but not out. There is an elaborate, but ineffectual program to prevent intrusion, but not much info goes out from the room. He seems to be storing it all on his hard disks. By the way, we got into the Foundation's computers. There's no sign of a connection to DeBoer's computer."

"No back up?" Ali asked.

"Maybe your computer tech can answer that question?" Red asked. "We think the back up is in the room on another hard drive."

I went back to the Club and went to talk with Luther. He looked frazzled. His men had gone off to take a load of equipment back to their office. He was alone. "They want the whole thing removed by tomorrow. The boss man told me to do it, and then said he was off to a vacation in Brazil," he complained. We later found out the boss never made it to the plane.

"No extradition treaty there," I remarked. Luther looked stunned.

"You know a lot more about this than you're telling me?" he asked. "Am I in deep do-do?"

"Let's go where we can talk," I said. We went to my bedroom. There I outlined what was going on.

"Am I the fall guy?" Luther asked.

"That may be, but I'm not sure," I said. "The thing fell apart so quickly. They may not have had a chance to work out a way to frame you. You're just a bystander as far as I can tell."

There was a knocking at my door. I opened it and it was Carlton. "I'm the manager now," he blurted out. "Rutherford cleared out his office and left without a forwarding address."

"The rats are leaving the ship," Luther said. I explained the situation to both men. It took only a few minutes to realize things were much easier now. Carlton had the keys for the club. We could get anything we wanted from DeBoer's room.

As we talked, I noticed that Luther and Carlton made eye contact and they liked what they saw. Luther's cell phone rang. His crew was in traffic and was going to get some dinner before they came back to the club. Luther told them he could handle things this evening and to go home. We went to DeBoer's room and Luther worked on the computer as I looked for disks. Luther knew his stuff. He hadn't set up the system, but had gone over the set up at his office and had a diagram. The central computer distributed storage to a series of external hard drives. These were comparatively small units each with 120 gigs of storage. There was a large server, but this was essentially a dummy.

If DeBoer unplugged an external drive, the system would reset itself and there would be no record of the drive existing. The computer and the server were clean should there be an investigation. Luther said this was a set up ideal for someone who wanted to collect illegal porn. The external drives were easily disposed of. Luther unplugged the drives. I found a box with a few hundred DVDs.

The DVDs were in packets of three. DeBoer labeled one packet Senator Thornhill. Inside DeBoer had labeled one disk, "Master," another was "Backup," and the third was "Thornhill's copy." I went through the box and found Willamette's packet. Only the master and the backup were there. That was clear enough. I found Johnson, the Admiral and Jack's packets. They were complete. DeBoer had not gone in for the kill. I looked for Abdul, and found nothing.

We removed all the incriminating evidence. Carlton was into housekeeping. He dusted and cleaned up the room, so we left no tell tale marks on the desktops. He also cleaned up fingerprints and rearranged the equipment so it would look undisturbed.

We took the drives and disks back to my room. Ali and Red were waiting. They had no problem getting in without a key. Carlton and Luther were a bit scared, but we got down to business quickly. Luther went over the set up and they looked at the drives. The next question was how to destroy them. We were all on the same side, but the information on the drives could be valuable, so valuable it might turn the heads of a spy organization.

Luckily, the club owned an old-fashioned incinerator. The EPA no longer approved this sort of a machine, but it still worked like new. Luther opened the hard drives and moved the hard disks. He had a strong magnet and erased the disks. We added those to the pile of disks and put them in the incinerator. The unit had three days of paper and trash in it and I cranked it up.

The disks vaporized and all the blackmail information converted into fumes that went up the chimney and floated over the rooftops of Washington. It was one in the morning now. Luther got another cell call. The truck had broken down. He told the men to go home and get another truck in the morning.

"We were supposed to get it done tonight, but I guess I'm the boss now," Luther said. "In a day or two I suspect I won't have a job, but I not too sure the company will be in existence anyway."

"I'd be a bit surprised if there is anything left in your company's bank accounts," Red said.

"Shit," Luther exclaimed, "You're damn right about that. The boss is off to Rio! He offered us a bonus to do the job tonight. I wondered why he was so generous. He's one tight bastard."

"Would anyone like a drink," I asked. "It can be a celebratory drink, or a way to drown your sorrows, depending on your personal situation." As part of my reward for catching the mugger, the ladies gave me cookies and brownies. Their husbands dropped off bottles of Old Crow and Southern Comfort. We all drank.

I'm not as young as I use to be and am experienced, but even now, I get surprised at the times when sex rears its head. Ali was tall, dark and handsome, but he was taking sly glances at Luther. Red seemed to be attracted to Carlton. I knew the sexual tastes of everyone but Ali and that was becoming clearer to me. After another drink or two, we were all getting mellow.

Much to my surprise Ali made the first move on Luther. Luther looked surprised, and then glanced at me. I winked at him. Luther went with the flow. Red got closer to Carlton and put his arm around the young man. I was wondering if I would be the odd man out. I laughed to myself at that thought. Once I was naked, somehow I always managed to have some fun.

I made another drink for the men. "It's late," I said. "You can either go home, or get naked and have some fun."

This time, Ali who looked surprised. "That's an easy decision," he said as he took off his shirt. We settled into a nice evening of no holds barred sex. Nude, Ali was an Arabian Bluto, very muscular and hairy. It was clear to me he wanted to fuck Luther. As far as I knew, Luther's ass was virgin until my experience with him earlier. Luther was an adult and I figured he would deal with it. Ali had a long, rather thin cock with a huge knob.

I just happened to notice Ali checking Luther's clothes as Luther stripped. Ali was a sly one. He was using this as a chance to check for additional disks. Ali also was rock hard by the time he was naked and he was already dripping.

Carlton was as un virgin as a man could be. He liked older men and Red hit the spot. They were both erect. Somehow, Carlton managed to have his ass hole open and accessible at all times. Red knew a bottom pig when he saw one. I went over to Carlton and Red since I figured they wouldn't mind a third. There was often an uncomfortable period between the time you get naked and real sex starts. That wasn't a problem here.

Luther was a sucker and swallowed Ali's cock as soon as it was in range. He was a good cocksucker and Ali appreciated his skills. Luther and Red were on my bed in the 69 position. Red was taller than Carlton so, while his cock was deep into Carlton's throat, Carlton's ass was within licking range.

Red took his time. He sucked the cock, and then the balls then his tongue wandered toward Carlton's hole. There was no resistance at all. I watched as Carlton reacted to the tongue probing his ass. I got next to them. Red held Carlton's legs back so he could adjust the height of the ass. When his hole was at my cock height, I moved in. Now Red had to make a choice between Carlton's hole and my cock head.

Red was at heart a diplomat. He licked the hole, then my head. I was revved up and Red would take the pre cum drooling from my slit with his tongue, and then work it into the quivering ass. He would spit to get more of my natural lubricant into the ass. Carlton began to moan.

Several times my cock head and Red's tongue shared the hole. Red had a long tongue. I finally popped my cock head though the sphincter. Carlton shivered in excitement. I pulled out and Red licked my head again.

"Peppermint!" he said. Carlton must have douched earlier, or fucked himself with a peppermint stick. I pushed deeper in his ass. There was no resistance.

"That looks good, doesn't it?" Ali said to Luther. I hadn't noticed they had come over to watch us.

"It sure as shit does," Luther said.

"Do you think you could do that?" Ali whispered.

"Take Noland's cock?"

"No, take my cock," Ali replied.

Luther looked Abdul in the eye and said, "I'd like to try." Carlton could have been the poster boy for anal sex. He loved it and you could tell. He shivered, shook and moaned with every thrust. I think he inspired Luther. I pulled out and let Red play for a while.

"What's the best way to do it?" Luther asked

"You just let me take charge," Ali said. "I know what works best."

"Okay," Luther said. I was sure Ali knew what was good for him, but not so sure he knew what would be good for Luther. I got out a tube of lubricant. Luther got on the bed next to Carlton and Abdul lifted the computer geek's legs onto his shoulders.

I lubricated Luther's ass. "Damn you're tight," I said.

"Don't worry, I'm strong," Ali said. "Once my gland is inside it will be easy." I was a bit uneasy.

Ali was right. He made a hard thrust and popped Luther's cherry in a split second. Ali stopped and let Luther adjust to the organ, and then he slowly pushed deep. He was three or four inches on the dark side of the sphincter when Luther relaxed and moaned. Ali's knob and Luther's nut met and fell in love. Strictly speaking, it may not have been love, but when the two organs caressed each other, it was damn close.

Ali was a surprise. He was a bruiser of a man, but turned almost kitten like once he was fucking. After a round of orgasms, I got to bed at 2:30 in the morning. All was well.

Luther returned to the club at 9:00 to remove the rest of the equipment. At about 9:15 he got a call from the company bookkeeper. The boss looted the company bank accounts. They were empty. Paul and Lonnie failed to appear at lunchtime, so Carlton pressed me into service as a waiter.

I heard a lot of gossip among the members. Rutherford had not been popular, and the older members disliked the newer men, especially DeBoer. I had a chance to call Mr. Willamette and told him of the progress. I explained why I had destroyed the records. "It may make it harder to find your son's killer," I said, "but it's the best for everyone in general." He agreed.

"Do you think you can find the man?" he asked.

"I'm not sure, but I'd like to work on it for another week," I said. "I bet there are a slew of uneasy men and something may fall our way." The big news that afternoon was of a car accident that killed DeBoer the night before. DeBoer apparently fell asleep at the wheel and his car drove over an embankment in the Catskills.

Offhand, this stuck me as either the most remarkable coincidence in history, or an outright murder. Either one of the victims of his scheme did it, or DeBoer wasn't the top man. I wondered if it was Hatfield, or Montague. Someone in the scheme needed protection, and DeBoer was a human sacrifice.

It seemed to me the later alternative was more likely. Commander Willamette had been a victim of DeBoer. It was more likely there was a kingpin. After I served dinner, I went off to my favorite Starbuck's for coffee. As I left the Club, Johnson appeared and joined me on the trek.

"You disturbed a hornet's nest," I said.

"I seem to have done that, but I have no idea why," Johnson said. "I thought the recording stuff was odd. Apparently, it was much more than odd. Do you know what's going on? You aren't want you seem to be, are you?"

"I'm not after you, if that's what you're worried about," I said. "I'm trying to find out who killed Commander Willamette. That's all."

"What about collateral damage?"

"As I told you before, if I had to destroy you to get my man, I wouldn't do it."

"Really?" Johnson said, and then he was silent for a while. "I'm not an admirable person in many ways. I've pandered to my base and I'm so deep in the closet, I can't see daylight anymore. Why would you protect me?"

"I come from a small town in rural Virginia," I explained, "There are lots of guys like you. In theory, they should know themselves better and be more honest about their sexual lives, but that's a hard thing to do when there's no one to support you, and you might destroy your life and everything you ever built. A murderer gets a trial. In many places, if someone exposes you as a gay man, there is no trial. You are guilty and get a life sentence."

"I don't know why those guys want to expose me," Johnson said. "We're on the same side. I'm just as conservative as they are."

"They're trying to sell second rate weapons and intelligence services to the government," I said. "It's about money. It's a scam."

"You're kidding? That can't be the case. They're all patriotic men."

"They're patriotic as long as patriotism is on the way to the bank," I said. "I wouldn't be surprised if their bank is off shore."

"I thought they were after my money," Johnson said. "I didn't think I had enough to amount to enough to be worth their while..."

"What committees are you on?"

"Oh shit," he exclaimed. "I do military appropriations."

"You haven't noticed you're not getting much for your dollar?" I asked. We were at the coffee shop so we stopped talking about the situation. Afterward, Johnson went off to his office. He was one unhappy man. A few days later Johnson ripped a new asshole in a Pentagon toady at a hearing. His questions followed those of a shrill but intelligent congress woman from California. Instead of giving the men a pass, Johnson continued her line of questioning and all but demolished the man who was lying to him. It was a shock. It was a new day.

Part 10

As far as I could tell, Red, who was a British agent and Ali, who worked for an Arab government, were the only ones interested in the case. There was no evidence the Metropolitan Police, or any entity associated with the U. S. Government, had any interest. The murder of a naval officer should have been a big deal. I wondered how high the plot extended into the government.

That morning Conrad returned to the shower room, early. The place was empty. He was nervous. We talked, but he didn't seem to be able to get to the point. After a few minutes, Jack appeared. Jack is a nice person, but didn't have the best genital control. He got half-hard when he saw Conrad and me. Conrad turned away and went to a shower in one corner of the room, trying to avoid looking at either me, or Jack. When he turned and looked at us, Jack had a full erection and I was on the high side of half-staff.

Conrad got hard in a second. He was shocked at what he saw, but too shocked to move. Jack looked uneasy too. Jack and Conrad were both handsome men, and were attracted to each other. The situation had all the makings of a porn writer's dream.

The dream took a step on the wild side a second or two later. Conrad's father, the Admiral, appeared. The Admiral was hard as a rock. We were all adults and there wasn't any question as to what was going on.

"Everybody here knows each other," I said. "I guess it's time for everyone to get to know each other better." I motioned for the men to get closer to me. We formed a quartet to the side of the shower.

"I know a lot of men who spend a good part of their life hiding their real nature from the people they love. This turns some men mean and others get bitter," I said. "The problem is that you can't fool Mother Nature. You are the way you are and pretending you aren't, or hiding behind a false personality doesn't change that."

"You are all good men who just happen to like other men," I continued. "It's not a freak of nature and it's not a judgment from God. Not one of you is mean, nasty, or hateful. I'm the best son a mother could ever have and the best friend you would ever want. It just happens that I'm a great cock sucker and ass fucker." There was silence.

"I've always thought Conrad was the best thing that ever happened to me," the Admiral said. "He's been a joy since the moment he was born. I feel the same about him now as it did at that moment."

I could almost feel years of fear and shame vanishing into thin air. Both men had lived in terror the other would discover their dark secret. Neither guessed they shared the same fears and the same secret. They hugged and then we all hugged.

"I've never been so relieved in my life," Conrad said. "I was so scared."

My cock touched their cocks as we embraced. "Damn you are hung like a horse!" the Admiral exclaimed.

We all laughed. "A friend of mine said I'd never get to be Mr. Universe, but if they had a Mr. Congeniality, I'd be a sure bet. I may be ugly, but my cock makes friends like all get out." Jack dropped to his knees and began sucking all three of us.

"I'm off to my bedroom," I said. "I'm not sure I can take another guy walking in on us." Jack and I dried off and left. About a minute after we got to the bedroom, someone knocked at my door. It was the Admiral and Conrad.

"Are we interrupting?" the Admiral asked.

"Hell no," I replied. They joined us.

"You may not believe this, but we're horny as hell," Conrad said. "It seems odd, but..."

"Have you two ever had sex without being afraid someone was going to discover you?" I asked. I knew the answer. "It's okay to enjoy sex and to enjoy another man's body. We're all adults. We all know what we like. Go with the flow."

They were ready. The Admiral paired off with Jack. Conrad and I renewed our acquaintance. This time the Admiral was a full participant, sucking Jack with relish and relief. I would bet he had wanted it for years. This was his first guilt-free physical contact with his lover's genitals. After a while, we traded partners. Jack and Conrad were soon connected, cock to mouth.

Conrad soon discovered Jack's preference for anal and had him on his hands and knees as he fucked him doggy style. The Admiral liked that a lot. I wasn't the Admiral's type, but we did well, very well. He liked Jack and loved his son. I was just another guy. He didn't need to be careful with me and he wasn't worried if I'd like him afterwards. Sex can be really good when you let go. He had a beer can style cock and bull balls. The balls were producing precum by the bucketful.

The Admiral would have preferred to be the calm and collected type, but his balls would have nothing of that. He had been holding back for most of his life and they wanted release. If you like men and like cocks, my cock can do a number on you. The look, the smell and the taste of an excited cock are the best aphrodisiac. Jack may have loaded the Admiral's sexual pistol, but my cock pulled the trigger.

After we had sucked like dogs in heat, we calmed down. The Admiral was standing watching Conrad deep dicking Jack as I played with his tits and rubbed my cock against his ass crack. The Admiral lost his load in a three-alarm orgasm. I often say good sex can be messy. His first ejaculation shot a ribbon of cum across Jack's body and spattered against Conrad's chest. The second and third shot hit the same place and dribbled down Conrad's treasure trail. Conrad collected the goo on his hand. He pulled his cock out of Jack's ass, coated it in his dad's cum and shoved it back in again.

By now his Dad's cum wasn't shooting as far and was landing on Jack's back. It was a sperm rainstorm. From the doggy position, Jack had a clear view of the spewing cock. By now the Admiral's cum splattered Conrad and Jack. A few seconds later Conrad popped, shooting his load deep in Jack's ass. Jack followed in a few seconds later. We all rested.

I asked if any of them knew anything about DeBoer's death. "You know there was a camera recording system in one of the rooms here?" I said.

"You're kidding?" Conrad said, obviously shocked. "Where was it?"

"In Room 8," I said. "It fed into DeBoer's room."

"That fucking bastard!" the Admiral exclaimed. "That's what was up. Those twerp waiters were always trying to get me to party in the carriage house. It was a blackmail scheme?"

"That what it looked like to me," I said. "DeBoer was running it, but it seems odd he had an accident at this time."

"Somehow DeBoer never impressed me as a leader of men," Jack said. "He struck me as a toady who made it a point to be near important men." It was getting late and the Admiral and Conrad had to leave.

Jack stayed and we talked for a while. Someone knocked at my door. It was Johnson. He was surprised to Jack lying naked on my bed, but he seemed to like the view. "I need to talk," he said.

"Come on in," I said. "We have an informal dress code here, but do join us."

"I don't know if I should," he stammered.

"We're all friends. Don't turn shy on me," I said. He entered the room, stripped and joined us on the bed. He had just heard of DeBoer's accident and it worried him.

"Was it an accident?" he asked.

"It's an awfully convenient accident," Jack said. "Quite a coincidence, I would say."

"That's the way I see it too," I said.

"This whole thing isn't nickel and dime stuff, is it?" Johnson asked. "I was thinking the take could easily involve millions."

"I think it may be in the billions. Do you know of any of DeBoer's associates? I know of a man named Hatfield and of Carl Montague, the preacher." I asked.

"I met both," Johnson said. "Hatfield runs something out west called God-Pac. It gives cash to Christian Candidates for office. Carl is their front man for fund raising and the head of the All America Foundation." Johnson said.

"Did you know Hatfield is on the board of the Enterprise Group?"

"You're kidding!" Johnson said. "He did say they were an up and coming security group. I had no idea he was involved."

"Did you get money from them or God-Pac?" I asked.

"No, I'm not Christian enough. They had a 20-point Declaration of Values you had to subscribe to get the cash. One of those points was to provide public funding for churches and church schools. They also wanted to require members of the armed forces to be Christian. I was opposed to those. Carl and Hatfield don't like any variation from the true path," Johnson said.

"I will bet he alone knows the true path?" I remarked.

Johnson looked at me. "I think that's right. Carl was the "spiritual" leader of God Pac; Hatfield was the Executive Director, but there was a vice President I didn't like at all, Andres Chance. He was odd. He talked about saving America. That wasn't so unusual, but I think his vision of saving involved reeducation camps and many arrests and what he called "rightful retribution." He let it slip that involved getting money to Christians from Jews and perverts."

"That has a nice Germany in 1933 feel to it," Jack said.

"It turned me off," Johnson said.

I told Jack and Johnson about my run in with Carl and the attempted rape. I'm not a kiss and tell man, but rape didn't count.

"You're kidding me!" Johnson exclaimed. "I can't believe it!"

"Well you have Jimmy Swaggart and the Bakkers," I said. "Ted Haggard liked gay sex as long as it was for pay. It's not that unusual. Being walled up in a closet can do strange things to a man."

"That would be my guess," Jack said. We talked about the scheme, but as we talked, the sexual tension in the room grew. I hadn't shot off yet, so I was still hard. Johnson was getting excited, as Jack recovered from his earlier climax.

As Johnson and I chatted, Jack leaned over and began to suck Johnson's cock. Johnson jumped a little, but relaxed. "I can't believe this is happening," he said. "I loved what we did the other day, but..."

"But what?" I asked.

"Do you guys need to fuck me?" he asked. "I got to fuck you. It seemed kind of one sided. What are the rules?"

I smiled. "You've got the right attitude, but the rules aren't that mechanical," I said. "I don't think sex has to be 50/50 all the time. Jack likes to bottom. You like to top. As long as you're both happy, all is well. Do you want to try to take a cock?"

"I don't really know. Is it as good as it seems?" Johnson asked.

Jack looked up from his cock sucking duties. "It is for me!" he said, smiling. I had a suspicion as to where this conversation was going, but it was getting late and I had to get to work. They left and I went to sleep. The next morning, no waiters had shown up again, so I pulled table duty. The air was thick with gossip at breakfast but none of it seemed credible to me.

Johnson's friend, Willard, was at lunch. He was the man who needed the yard work, got me to agree come by his house that weekend to make recommendations as to what he should do in his garden. I wasn't sure what that was about, nor did I know how well he knew Johnson. Willard was a short, massive unkempt man who always looked as if he had just rolled out of bed after a bad night. He seemed cheerful. He often lunched at the club and worked at a think-tank. He and his companion at lunch had been talking about DeBoer's death and they seemed to know him well.

"I was surprised he died alone," Willard said. "He told me he was meeting with Hatfield and another high roller who was going to contribute to his foundation. I thought they were to be meeting at about the time DeBoer died." The other man suggested Beltway traffic held up DeBoer. That meant nothing. Everyone in D.C. blames the beltway. It's the traditional explanation for every delay.

I drove out to a wealthy suburb along the Potomac that evening. I went into a gated community; the guard okayed me by the gate and went past a slew of MacMansions before I reached Willard's over-grown house.

He lived in an old farmhouse. Apparently, the development was on his former farm. The house itself was handsome, nice and in good condition. A young Mexican let me in. Willard appeared a minute later. The contrast between the house and the property was striking since the house was in top-notch shape.

"It's good of you to come," Willard said. "As you can tell, the place got away from me. My wife was the gardener and when she died, so did most of the garden." We went out and wandered around. It had been nice.

"I'd love to help you out, but this is a bigger project than I can do, single handed," I said. "You need a crew."

"Actually, I have a crew," Willard said. "Pablo, would you get your father?" he asked of the Mexican. A minute or two later, an older Mexican appeared. "Clydesdale, this is Jesus. He takes care of the property. I just hired one of his cousins to be my yardman. Jesus comes complete with three sons, so I have the labor force. I just need direction. I was hoping you could spend a day and give him some pointers." I shook hands with Jesus.

"Actually, I thought Pablo might replace Tyrone at the club," Willard said.

"I'm sorry I got his job. It was a spur of the moment thing," I said.

Willard laughed, "It was no problem at all," he said. "Pablo could fill Tyrone's shoes in some ways, but not in the garden. I am reliably informed you more than fill the need. You've done wonders for Johnson."

We weren't talking about gardening. Jesus was a good-looking man in his forties and his sons ranged from being cute to drop dead handsome. They clearly weren't all his children. One was almost his age and another was black. It was getting dark, so I left, but agreed to spend Saturday there. I wasn't at all sure what Willard was after, but had a good sense it involved more than gardening.

The rest of the week was uneventful. The mystery of the missing waiters continued. Both Lonnie and Paul had vanished. Carlton got a call from Lonnie's mother looking for him. Carlton called them in as missing persons, but the police weren't too worried about missing gay hookers. I was more worried about finding their bodies. Carlton hired temporary waiters so I got out of the dining room.

On Saturday, I drove back to Willard's house. Jesus and Pablo knew shit about gardening, but they learned fast. His boys were hard workers and after a morning's work, the outline of the garden was visible again. Willard was all but jumping with joy.

"Lunch is waiting in the barn," Willard announced. Two of Willard's friends joined us for lunch. "This is Gus, and the hot jock is Don. Gus was dapper and preppy. Don was my size, but was well built. He looked military with his crew cut and had a strong Southern accent. It sounded like Alabama to me. We had lunch in a barn. The barn was off to the side of the property and I hadn't paid any attention to it. From the outside, it looked like an old building, but when I went inside, I realized it was modern and contained a swimming pool.

It was a crisp, cool day, but I had worked up a sweat. I was a little surprised that Jesus and his boys joined us for lunch. "Everyone take a dip and then we'll eat," Willard announced. The Mexicans stripped naked and jumped in the pool. Willard and his friends stripped quickly. I was the last one in.

There was one overarching characteristic of Jesus, Pablo and the boys; all were endowed. By the time we got out of the water, they were all at least semi-erect. None of them looked uneasy; no one had any problem being naked.

At lunch, one of the Mexicans sat next to each of us and it was almost as if Willard assigned them to a guests. We had beer with lunch and after a few brews, the atmosphere got more relaxed. Gus looked slightly familiar. When he spoke, I realized he was a television reporter, Augustus Miller. I recognized the voice, if not the man. The men weren't shy about their endowment. All were checking out the other men's equipment.

Willard was built like a gorilla and had a beer can cock. Pablo sat next to him. Gus, the reporter, was middle aged. He was blond and had a swimmer's body. He had a long, thin cock and big, low hanging balls. Willard, Don and he were the only cut men in the group. Two of the youngest Mexican's, Luis and Roberto, were next to him. Both of them were mostly of Mayan ancestry. They were hairless except for thick pubic bushes. One had a cock that curved up when he got excited, the other's cock curved down. They were close to being fully erect all the time.

The back man, Carlo, sat next to Don. He was a muscleman, with curly, black hair on his chest. His complexion was golden brown, but his cock and balls were huge and black. Carlo also had a Jamaican accent and was very outgoing and cheerful. I got the feeling sitting next to a naked black man was a new experience for Don. Don shaved his body except for a cube of hair at his pubic region. His had a fire-plug style cock and big balls. Carlo was so friendly, Don warmed up quickly.

I sat with Jesus. Jesus was short, very muscular and hairy. He was uncut and his cock head peaked out from the skin depending on how excited he was. The skin was dark, but his cock head was apricot sized, pink and dripped precum. It was a pretty sight.

I glanced at Jesus' sons and asked, "Did you start having children when you were three or four years old?"

He laughed. "It would be better to say we are all members of the same brotherhood," he said. "Apparently, it was mistranslated when they immigrated here. Where we come from, it can be bad for members of our fraternity. Willard helped me get away and we help other men such as ourselves when the opportunity arises."

"How many men have you helped?" I asked.

"Several dozen," Jesus said. "All get jobs and move out quickly."

"Are your sons and cousin going to move away?" I asked.

Jesus leaned next to me and whispered, "These men like it here. Willard is a good man and they enjoy him. He's very accommodating. He likes big men. He can take them for hours."

"All of you enjoy him?" I asked.

Jesus nodded. "That's why we're all here. His taste and our sex drives match," he said. "His friends are nice too, uninhibited."

"Why am I here?" I asked.

Jesus smiled. "I bet you know why!" he said. "I hope you aren't offended."

"I'm not offended, but a bit surprised," I said.

"You made quite the impression at the club," Jesus said. "You have all of Tyrone's assets without the attitude." I glanced at Willard. Pablo was playing with his cock as he talked to Gus. One of the young men was sucking Gus's cock while the other stroked his own cock. Don was playing with Carlo's meat. Jesus and I were the only ones who were not playing. That didn't last for long. Jesus fondled my cock.

"Noland," Willard said. "A little birdie told me you were the one who pulled the plug on the Mandrake Club movie studio."

"I did mention I noticed some odd equipment in one of the rooms," I said. "It kind of puzzled me."

"Did you notice who use to visit the room?" Gus asked.

"I'm new at the club so I don't know the names," I said.

"Would you recognize the men if you saw photographs?" he asked.

"No chance in hell," I said.

"Fair enough," Gus said. "I had to try. It's the reporter's code. I'm not into outing guys." That was obvious. The two younger men were working on his cock. It cock was long and thin and the men took turns deep throating him. Gus was open-minded.

"I heard the studio's offices were in another room at the club," Don said. "The room that guy who died stayed in?"

"Strange he had an accident, isn't it?" I said. Don looked at me. "Quite a coincidence," I added. "I wonder who his playmates were."

"Sexual playmates?" Willard asked.

"I was thinking about his business partners," I said.

"Really?" Don asked.

"Follow the money," I said. "I admit chasing a cock is more fun than chasing the money, but someone went to a lot of trouble with the recording system. Money's involved. It's too fancy for a little titillation."

"I'm not into little titillations," Willard said. Everyone burst out laughing. Everyone was hard and everywhere you looked, there was an impressive piece of meat. "This conversation has been really interesting, but if I don't get a cock in my ass, I going to explode."

"I thought you'd never get to the point!" Gus exclaimed.

"Don, Noland, we're all old friends here. Do either of you have a problem with a little anal fun?" Willard asked.

"It doesn't look to me as if there's any little anal here," Don said. "I'm a top. Is that a problem?"

"I wouldn't worry about that, "Willard said. "Our only rule is to ask before you poke."

"I do it all, but the top is my strong suit," I said. "I like sloppy seconds, after the hole has been stretched. Does that bother anyone?"

"Shit, I've died and gone to heaven," Willard moaned. All was well. As it turned out, all was more than well. I later found out Willard had slipped a dose of Viagra into the food. Not only was everyone fully erect, a single orgasm wasn't enough to lose your erection. The cock is the gift that keeps on giving, but this was especially true this afternoon.

Everyone was into fucking big time and everyone was versatile, except for Don. Don wasn't 100% truthful about that. Once he was revved up, I guessed he would be full service. It was a new experience to be in an all anal group. They all liked it and they weren't afraid to show it.

When I said, everyone was versatile, that didn't include Willard. He was a pure bottom, although pure might not be the best word to describe him. Purity had nothing to do with him. He loved it and never got tired of taking cock after cock. Pedro was the first to fuck him, but everyone had a chance.

No one here was a virgin, and Jesus let me know he wanted to be fucked. He was tight, so I took my time. I needed a shoehorn to get it in, but it was well worth the effort. Once I got in, he relaxed. I was slow stoking his ass when Carlo began to open my ass. He was filling. Carlo was more than six feet tall, so he had to scrunch down to get in my ass.

When Carlo was fully lodged in my ass, he stood up and lifted my legs off the floor. I was suspended between Jesus' ass and Carlo's cock. Carlo bounced me and I went deeper into Jesus' hole. Our little trio fell apart and Don took my place in Jesus' ass. I jumped into the pool to cool off. When I got out, I joined Gus, Willard and Pablo.

Part II

I'm not much of an asshole man. I like the way they feel as my cock slips deep into the ass, but I never think of as ass hole as pretty. A hole is just a hole. I have to admit I do feel some affection for the sphincter and even more for the prostate. I use to think the sphincter was just the dumb doorman who was trying to keep me out, protecting the crown jewel of the ass, the prostate.

Over the years, I've spent a lot of time muscling my way past the sphincter, or tricking it into opening. When things are going well, the sphincter turns into a natural cock ring, massaging my shaft while it works its magic on the prostate. At one time, I thought of the prostate as a sexual punching bag. Now it's more of a partner. I spend much more time caressing it with my cock than ramming it like a pile driver.

Willard and his friends were 100% anal in their interests. My experience with them gave me a new outlook on ass holes. At first, I thought the younger men were there as toys for the older men. It was soon apparent the younger men were full participants. They liked to plug and be plugged. Willard was a bottom, but everyone else was full service. Willard was either on his back or on his hands and knees.

I was the last of the group to screw him and was afraid he would have lost his muscle tone from the multiple penetrations. By the time I slid my cock into his hole, the ass was bloated and abused pillow of flesh, covered in lube and cum. Willard must have been taking anal aerobics for years. His ass all but kissed my cock as I pushed it in. He had firm sphincter muscles and an all but prehensile ass. As I fucked, he massaged my cock.

It was so tight earlier deposits of cum squeezed out as I pushed in, but Willard was happy and got happier the deeper I pushed. Willard was shivering after a few minutes of thrusting. Some men like to do virgins. They want to be the first into a man's ass and introduce him to the joys of hard-core sex. I know of some coaches who like that. The first time can be painful, but when the fucker is your coach, a man you have fantasized about for years, it can be good.

By no stretch of the imagination was Willard a virgin. He was near his limit. I like it when you play with a man who has some mileage on him and remind him what it was like to be young again. I'm sure he had taken bigger cocks than mine, or at least a dildo as big as mine, but a flesh and blood cock is different. A bloated organ, oozing cock juices and being on the edge of a climax can work magic.

Willard was on his hands and knees, so I had straddled him in a wide stance. I had noticed no one in the group tried to hide his hole. When possible everyone spread his cheeks. I figured, when in Rome do as the Romans. Gus came up behind me and nosed his organ into my hole.

Carlo had already opened me up. So when Gus came knocking at the back door, I was ready. It was easy to take, but more than did the trick. I was pretty keyed up already. Gus slipped in, pulled out some and then pushed deeper. I'm not sure what he hit, but it was a home run.

I suddenly needed to shoot my load. Somehow, Gus had both pulled the trigger, but Willard plugged the barrel. I was trapped in that few seconds between the beginning of my orgasms and the actual release. I was shaking as I had all the sensations of ejaculating, without shooting. Willard tightened his ass and trapped my cum in the piss tube. I was trapped in never-never land until Gus let loose and gave my prostate a sperm bath. The spurting cum in my ass was enough to push me over the edge. Willard released his grip and I flooded his innards with cream. I had a spectacular orgasm, as did Willard.

We broke apart and took a swim to cool down. Soon the rest of the group joined us and we played like school kids. Don was uneasy with the ethnic variety at the party, but had relaxed considerably. I'm not sure he had encountered anyone as open to being fucked as Carlo. Carlo looked like the B Movie Mandingo, but had no attitude at all. Before the swimming interlude, Don had fucked Carlo and then moved on to Jesus.

By now, everyone had shot off a few times. This was good for Don and his hang-ups. A big black guy with a rock-hard cock, who is looking at your ass hole, is the stuff of pornographic dreams. No one was more than semi-erect now and the cocks looked relaxed and less intimidating.

I assumed Don was a Federal agent of some type, FBI or the like. He had the up-tight, straight arrow look I associated with them. After the swim, Don, Jesus and Carlo stayed together. I joined them. They got along well, but there was still a little tension in the air. It all emanated from Don.

I have a nose for lust and sexual tension. I could smell it. He said he was a top, but I was sure he was thinking about expanding his repertoire. I suspected he was one of those men who thought being fucked was unmanly. Don was the kind of man who wanted to be in control. Once a cock is in your ass, your ability to control is low to non-existent.

That being said, I knew he wanted to give anal a spin. Everyone else in the group seemed to swing both ways and obviously enjoyed it. It might have been different if anyone tried to pressure him into bottoming. He wasn't the kind who would give in. He had to come to the decision himself.

I head the ring of a cell phone. It was Don's phone. He answered it and hastily left with Gus. The rest of us dressed and returned to the garden. I thought the long lunch would have left the men lethargic, but it seemed to have the opposite effect. It was a hot afternoon, but that didn't affect the Mexicans.

At first, I thought there would be issues between Willard and his boys. There was none. I thought it was a master and his sex toys relationship. It was more correctly a relationship between a savior and the saved. As it turned out, Willard was the sex toy, not the Mexicans. Jesus was the actual savior, since "adopting" them was his idea. Willard made it work. He was the overruling father figure. For a moment, I thought of looking for a Holy Ghost figure, but I abandoned that search quickly.

I talked with Willard and got his personal story. Willard had been part of DeBoer's and Dr. Carl Montague's odd circle of friends. When his wife died, Willard had a personal crisis. Carl appeared to support him. "He had all the answers," Willard said. "I have always been attracted to men, but was deeply in love with my wife. After her death, I was afraid I'd act on my gay preferences. I thought Carl could save me from that."

"I take it, that didn't work?"

"Not one bit. I found Jesus. The Mexican Jesus, not the one in heaven," Willard said. "Oddly I have had a few heavenly experiences with him."

"I noticed."

"Carl didn't save me the way I thought he would," Willard said. "He did liberate me from a cool million dollars."

"You seem okay with that," I said. I'd be pissed as hell."

"I'm an adult. I should have known better," Willard replied.

"Do you know of a man named Andres Chance?"

"I see you have a taste for bottom feeding," Willard remarked. "When I met Andres for the first time, I began to wonder about Carl Montague. He combines a paranoid view of the world with intense avarice. That's a very unattractive combination. Anders views Christianity as a money making scheme. Carl and Anders were tick as thieves and "thieves" is the right word."

"Would he have any problem ripping off the military?"

"He would regard that as an obligation. He loves the United States dearly; it just happens it isn't our United States. His United States doesn't include any blacks, Mexicans, or Jews. His United State is Christian, Republican and everyone knows his place. Notice I didn't say his or her place. Women have only one place, that is to stay home and keep house, cook and breed,"

"Carl seems to be content with forced sex."

"He has a strange approach to that. Sex is pure and only done for reproductive purposes, but it okay to support small business," Willard said.

"He supports small business such as hookers or gigolos?" I asked.

Willard laughed. "l hadn't thought of it that way, but it's close to being true. There is a big emphasis on submitting to the leader. Carl told me a woman wasn't truly a woman unless she had taken the sperm of a true Christian."

"Well he jumped me, or at least tried to jump me."

"Maybe he thought an injection of Christian sperm would turn me straight?"

Willard burst into laughter again. "That might actually be possible. Carl's ability to rationalize was remarkable. I'm not entirely sure how many straight cocks end up in the ass of a gay man."

"Maybe it is a straight cock with a bend toward the gay?" I suggested. Our conversation went downhill from there. I left Willard's at six, called my office, and asked them to do a search on Andres and more checking on Carl.

When I got back to the club, I saw Carlton. He was the acting director of the club, and was overwhelmed. Being a leader of men wasn't his strong suit. He was born to be an assistant manager. He told me the board had hired three new waiters to replace the ones that vanished, and a new director was on the way. "DeBoer's room has already been taken."

"Who has it now?" I asked.

"A smarmy guy named Andres Chance." Carlton replied. "He apparently was a pal of the late lamented DeBoer and had first dibs on the room. The new executive director visited yesterday. He's named Edwyn Wilson, with Edwin spelled with a "y." He strikes me as a martinet, but that may be first day on the job nerves."

The next day I met two of the new waiters, Troy and Lawrence. They were young, gay and horny. For our older members they were a dream come true. Troy looked like the grandson of your dreams, cute, polite and willing to suck. Lawrence affected a coy shyness that went over well.

The new director arrived full time the next day. He came with Andres. We had a brief staff meeting to do introductions. I got the impression Andres was his patron. Edwyn would have been a horrible actor. He couldn't even pretend to be interested in the staff. I guessed Edwyn's attitude toward people was entirely based on their rank. After a few days on the job, it ranged from contemptuous distain for the staff and fawning politeness for older, wealthier members. He was officiously polite to Andres, and unwilling to look a staff member in the eye, with the notable exception of Troy and Lawrence. I saw the third waiter for the first time, Tony. I think he many have been Mexican.

Poor Carlton immediately found his workload was unchanged. Edwyn didn't deal with the day-to-day operations of the club. He was above that. Andres didn't notice me, or anyone else on the staff was alive, with the exception of the new waiters. That was good for me.

The next day, I saw Troy leaving Chance's room at 6:00 in the morning. I didn't think it was a romantic tryst. I saw Troy and Lawrence chatting with Andres in the corners and back corridors. They were working for him. I also discovered Room 8 wasn't going to become a member's room; it would remain as a spare room for guests. I saw Troy with an older member visiting it after lunch.

I couldn't believe Chance was resurrecting the same scheme. It was like an instant replay. The collapse of DeBoer's operation didn't make a ripple in public. There was no mention of it in the press. Red and several parts of Naval Intelligence were on the trail, but as far as I could tell, as yet the FBI and the Metropolitan Police weren't involved.

I was under a bush in the garden trying to fix a sprinkler head when I overheard Andres on his cell phone.

"The plan was perfect, no one could have found out about it. DeBoer was a fool. He panicked when he made a mistake. He should have left everything in place. It was DeBoer, not the plan that went bad. I've checked our sources in the FBI. They don't have a clue," he whined. There was a pause and then he spoke again. "The new boys are good, Edwyn picked them well. If you want to have it done right, you have to do it yourself." He walked away and I couldn't hear any more.

Apparently, Andres had no knowledge the scheme had been found out. He may have been one of those men who aren't capable of admitting a mistake, not to mention failure. DeBoer had failed, not the plan. It was an incredible stroke of luck.

Johnson, my Congressman friend had moved out of the club and taken an apartment. An upper level Defense Department man took his room. He was an undersecretary of some sort. Edwyn, Andres and the new waiter had no interest in me, but the Under Secretary noticed me. The under secretary had unusual hours, and exercised late at night, the same time I was supposed to shower.

He heard me showering can looked in to see who was there. I later found out he was shy and modest and was uneasy about being naked in public. Fortunately, my cock caught his fancy. I don't think he consciously would have looked at me if he could have avoided it. His natural instincts were too strong. He just looked the first night. The next day he got up enough nerve to shower with me. He got under a showerhead at the other end of the shower room. I know a man in need when I see him. I washed my hair with my eyes shut to give him some gawking time.

I then took a long time drying off. He came in to dry off and get dressed, and I introduced myself. I explained I had a room next to the exercise space as part of my pay. He said his name was Jameson Todd. Jameson was average in most ways. I guessed he was in his early 40s, balding and borderline pudgy. As is often the case with bald men, he had more hair on his chest than on his head.

"Are you the only man here?" he asked.

I said yes. "No one ever shows up late. After 11:00 this place is as private as your own bathroom."

"Are you they only staff member who uses it?" he asked. I nodded.

"The water pressure in my room is low," he observed. He tried to be casual.

"Are you the new man in Johnson's room?" I asked. "He had problems with it too. The water down here is fine." I pulled shorts on and went to the exercise room. He went back to doing his exercise routine. After ten minutes, he went to the locker room, and shortly thereafter, I heard the shower.

I went to the door and locked it. I went to the shower. "The place is officially closed so I locked the door," I said. "You can let yourself out; it's not locked from the inside."

His back was to me and he said, "Thanks." He turns slightly and I caught a glimpse of his erect organ. I dropped my shorts and joined him in the shower. He was a tightly wound spring. I sensed the tension in the air.

"Can I help you wash your back?" I asked. He whispered, "Yes."

Jameson shivered when I touched him. I briefly washed his back, but soon reached around and washed his chest with one hand and his balls with the other.

"Is it safe here?" he whispered.

"The door is locked," I said, "It's safe." He was hard. "Have you ever had fun in a shower room?"

"No," he said. "I've thought about it though. I was in high school I was afraid I would show hard I was so excited." I felt his cock and his cockhead was slippery. He turned around and dropped to his knees. He just stared at my cock. "Damn, it's big. What do you do with it?

"The usual things," I said. "That sort of depends on you."

"Can guys take it? In the ass, I mean."

"Some men can, it they want it bad enough."

He finally leaned forward and licked my knob. Jameson concentrated on my cock had then gradually open his mouth wider and took more of the organ.

"I like to sixty-nine. Are you good with that?" I asked.

"I'm afraid I'll shoot off," he said.

"That's fine with me, I wouldn't mind sampling your home brew."

"I've never taken another man's cum."

"I understand. You are as used to thinking of your cock as an organ to aim your piss; it's a mental leap to sucking on it as a man seed spigot. I think of cum as a reward for a job well done. Don't worry, I'll warn you when I'm close," I said. I turned off the water and we went to the locker area.

"Get on a bench and I'll straddle you." I said. Jameson was obedient. I straddled him with my cock at his mouth and mine just below my mouth. When I took his cock into my mouth he shot a volley of sperm on my tongue. "Slow down and try to control it, relax. Jameson was a born follower. He did exactly what I told him to do. He held back.

An aborted orgasm is rare but fun to play with. Sometimes it's like playing with a loaded gun. The man is on the edge, his cock head is ultra sensitive and tender. Other times, it reduces the urge to climax and the guy is ready for overtime. Jameson was of the later sort. He relaxed and enjoyed it.

While he held back the sperm, he couldn't hold back pre cum. It was sweet, slippery and tasty. I like precum anyway, but his must have included a special ingredient. They say its function is as a lubricant, but it can be an aphrodisiac for me. I'm into sex anyway but Jameson's ball juices got me going big time. It was hot.

Jameson had seemed so shy I was afraid he might be one of those men who is responsive as rock. He was reserved, but my cock in his mouth and his in mine got him into the game. It was good for both of us.

I got close to shooting so we pulled apart. "Are you okay?" I asked.

"More than okay," he replied. "It's never been this good."

"Are you regretting all those opportunities you missed in the High School shower room?"

"I wouldn't have had enough nerve to do that then," he said. "I thought I was the only gay guy in the school. I did know anyone else felt the way I did."

"We all felt that way," I said. He was flat on his back on the bench with his cock sticking straight up. I swung a leg over the bench, straddled him, and then sat on it. He was oozing so much precum the entry was effortless.

"Jesus!" he cried.

"The name is Clydesdale," I replied. I'm afraid my warm and welcoming ass caressing his love stick was too much for him. He didn't notice my humor. His cock was a thin curved shaft with a big mushroom. My prostate took an immediate fancy to the knob. I squeezed my ass and Jameson moaned in pleasure. He loved it.

I knew he was ripe and ready to blow. I did a little dance on his cock to see if that would get him off. It didn't, so I had some fun. I decided to see what a tight sphincter and a warm ass could do. Jameson had limited experience as a top, and my ass introduced him to a new level of feeling. Technically, he fucked me, but it was more correct to say my ass masturbated his cock. I was shocked at his stamina. He was near an orgasm at all times, but he held off shooting for at least ten minutes.

When he finally shot off it was a prizewinner. I was sitting on his cock and hand a hard time holding him down as he bucked and twitched with each ejaculation. He all but passed out due to the intensity. It was more than a sperm bath of my prostate; he lubricated my rectum with his steamy sperm.

"I didn't know it could be that good," he moaned.

"I had a suspicion you liked it. It was good for me too. I like long sessions."

"I didn't mean to shoot in you," he said. "I'm sorry. I've never done that before. I'm tired. I need to get to bed." I got up and his cock slipped out of my hole. He was still hard, so I sat on it again and squeezed my ass really tight to get the last drops of cum from him.

"I can't take it anymore," he cried. I didn't think he was entirely sincere about that, so I did it a few more times and then let him go. He was a bit dizzy so I helped him up. He went to his room. I went to sleep.

Part 12

The next day I had an interesting conversation with Tony, one of the new waiters. I had thought he looked Latino, but he was Lebanese. With curly black hair and an olive complexion he wasn't as pink and twinky as the other waiters. He was cute and perky, but he actually had hair on his chest. Unlike the other waiters, he wasn't afraid of me and actually got a long with Roosevelt, the black headwaiter.

I think Edwyn made a mistake selecting Tony. Tony was gay as a goose and loved sex, but he was naturally friendly and out-going. The other two needed the prospect of a cash incentive to be attracted to a man. Troy just liked sex with older men. Much to my surprise, he thought I was an older man. I never thought of myself as an older guy, but that wasn't the way Troy saw it. He looked older than the other waiters' looked, but was twenty. They looked boyish, but he was ten years younger than the bois.

He had the sex drive of a bull, and was ready, willing and able to get it on whenever the occasion permitted. He was also a size queen, thus his interest in Roosevelt and me. Roosevelt never played with waiters under his supervision. He knew that was a recipe for disaster. Tony never got to play with Roosevelt's black snake, but Tony was satisfied just being near it. Tony saw it when they were at the urinals. Tony made a pass and Roosevelt politely declined. He told Tony if he liked them big he might strike up a conversation with me.

Tony's goal in life was to become a personal trainer. He was muscular and buffed. Edwyn let him try out for the role in the exercise room, between his stints as a waiter. He was at the room after lunch for two hours and from eight-thirty to ten at night. He was good at that and the club members like him. He was just demanding enough for them to feel they got some real exercise, but not so demanding to be a pest. Tony wore clothes that were form fitting, but not overtly sexual. He wore shorts and a tank top, but no jock. If you were doing sit ups on the floor, you would periodically get a view of his equipment. That was very popular.

Tony knew I used the locker room showers, and as a staff member, I wasn't supposed to shower when members were using the room. When then last member left he came over to my room and told me the showers were available. Surprise of surprises, when I went to shower a few minutes later he was still there, working on one of the exercise machines.

I went to the shower and turned the water on. He appeared next to me. "Damn, Roosevelt said you were a big boy," he said.

"You like that?" I asked.

"How big is it hard?" he asked. Tony wasn't into subtlety much.

"It gets quite a bit bigger," I said, "But I hate to get it up and not have a way to drain it." I wasn't going to win any awards for subtlety either. "My balls are fully loaded." Tony tried to deep throat it then and there. I was still soft so he got it all in his mouth. He had experience sucking cock, but as my meat grew, he had to give it up, reluctantly. We went to my room. It goes without saying; I like size queens. Tony was as enthusiastic and willing as any I had met.

He liked sex with older men, but he wasn't looking for a sugar daddy. He liked the cream from your cock, not the cash in your wallet. He sported seven inches of uncut cock, meaty, but not massive. Unfortunately, he had a tight ass. I would work on that later.

Tony loved to suck, I just got on my bed and let him do the work. I asked if he had a problem with cum in his mouth. He said, "Not with your cum." He was true to his word. We chatted when he needed a break.

"How did a nice boy like you end up here?" I asked.

"The money is good. I was working at a Ponderosa and one of my buds told me a guy was looking for waiters," Tony said. "My bud was a friend of Lawrence. He called Lawrence and got me an interview with Mr. Wilson. He old, like you, and I like that. The interview was at his apartment. He noticed I was checking him out and we ended up in his bed. He was into fucking and I didn't have much experience with that. His cock is okay, but quite thin. It felt good and he loved my ass. I actually got off hands free. Mr. Wilson loved that. I got the job."

"Do you want mine in your ass?"

"I'd love it in theory."

"A good answer," I said, laughing. "Have you ever been fucked silly?"

"Nope, but I am willing," he replied. "The men here are nice, but most shoot off before I got up to speed. One man shot off in my hand when I touched him. That was sort of neat. It's nice to be appreciated."

"You like older men?"

"I sure do. My Dad died when I was five. I can barely remember him. My Mom and her Sisters raised me, so it was always exciting when my Uncles visited and played with me."

"Was it sexual play?" I asked.

"Shit no. They weren't that kind of people," Tony answered. "I loved it when they visited. I didn't go to college and got a waiting job. I ran into a couple of guys there. One picked me up after work and took me home. He was a nice man and he showed me the ropes. I loved it."

"I bet he loved it too."

"I told him it was my first time. He was absolutely straight with me. Alex told me what he was doing and said he could stop any time I wanted," Tony continued. "My mom told me not to get a girl in trouble. They didn't say anything about having some fun with men. I didn't come close to guessing anything could be as good as sex was with Alex. Once I discovered man sex, I got into it big time. I can't get enough of it."

"Do you play with Edwyn often?"

"No, he's really into Troy and Lawrence," Tony replied. "Troy told me he likes Edwyn because he doesn't stretch his hole and shoots fast. He says the members like a virgin. One man told him he has a sweet ass and didn't know it was Edwyn's cum that made it so easy to penetrate."

"Does anyone play with Mr. Chance?"

"I don't know," Tony said. "He's not the friendliest person here. Troy and Lawrence seem to talk to him often, but I don't know what they talk about. He came here to exercise. Mr. Chance has a thick cock, but short. It's almost as thick as yours is. It would stretch Troy's ass. Lawrence told me he heard Mr. Chance telling Edwyn he thought I was too old for the job. Edwyn told him the members liked me."

"He likes his boys young. Maybe you can't play the blushing virgin as well as they can," I suggested.

"That may be it," Tony replied. "I've got to go; I'm doing breakfast tomorrow. Can we do this again?"

"Any time you're in the mood," I said.

The next morning I talked with Carlton. I told him I had run into Tony.

"I think he's a good kid," Carlton said. "He knows how to work. The other boys are good about chitchat, but can't get the food on the table in a reasonable time. He can serve half the room and the others take a quarter. Edwyn likes them. Mr. Chance doesn't like Tony at all."

"Maybe Tony's serving tables and the others are providing other services?"

Carlton didn't answer but he nodded. He leaned close to me. "They are getting blatant about it. I hate to say it but Lonnie was subtle compared to these guys. Troy is overtly flirting with some of the members."

"Andres Chance is supremely self-confident," I think. "I think he's always right and can't consider any alternatives." Carlton shook his head and walked off.

Earnest Hatfield arrived for a visit that afternoon. I was playing parking lot attendant, since the regular guy was getting to be more unreliable. He came in a cab from the airport and had a dispute with the Taxi driver. I had to pay the man, since Hatfield "knew" he was being over charged. Some club members were prone to forget to take cash so there was cash for the attendant to handle it. The club added these charges to their bill. I also had to be the bellboy, since Hatfield was way too important to carry his own bags. He wasn't the "could you help me with my bags type."

"Take my bags to my room," he ordered.

"And which room would that be?" I asked.

I could see him mouthing the words, "You fucking fool," but then he realized it was a reasonable request. "Room 8," he said. He had a trunk full of bags and the Taxi Driver wasn't going to help, so I got baggage carrier and loaded it up. His bags were either unusually heavy or very light. One suitcase contained clothes, but the others were a mystery. Noting rattled and it occurred some might be electronics packed in Styrofoam. The heavy bag could have contained a desktop computer.

I took his stuff to room 8, but I didn't have the key so I had to wait for him. He was pissed as hell when he saw me waiting. "Why didn't you unload the stuff?" he screamed.

"You have the key, Sir," I replied. Room 8 had an electronic key that changed with each user. He put is card in the lock and opened the door.

After I got the stuff in I asked, "Would you like me to help you un pack?"

He looked genuinely shocked at the thought. "Shit no, get out of here."

Hatfield was a prince among men. I left. There was no tip. When I got back to the parking area, the regular attendant finally appeared. "My alarm didn't work," he said. I hadn't had lunch so I went to a little sandwich shop nearby.

Red was there. There was a little park area across the street and we went there to talk. "I have some information for you this time," Red said. "Mr. Hatfield's corporation is a paper confection linking a multitude of newly minted entities providing arms and intelligence to the government. One or two of these entities have gone from annual gross receipts of $300,000.00 a year to over $600,000,000.00 in a two year period."

"Nice growth rate, they must have some very happy stockholders," I remarked.

"They seem to be owned by a small group of men, some of whom you may know," Red said. "One of their officers recently had an accident and died."

"Was it an accident in the Catskills?"

"This may shock you, but you guessed correctly," Red continued. "Rather oddly the corporation runs like a tontine. The survivor inherits all the assets of the departed. Even more oddly, the corporation was able to create this vast increase in receipts without increasing the staff. The corporation has four employees."

"That works out to $150,000,000.00 per person?"

"Yes, they apparently are most productive," Red remarked. "The whole thing is in the black budget, not accessible to public or congressional scrutiny. All their assents are in off shore banks. There is one wonderful aspect to the scheme. All the reports and analysis are done in India, apparently by under employed English majors who have a taste for old James Bond novels."

"How did you find this out?"

"We didn't. In spite of the James Bond things, Her Majesty's Government has some standards. It seems His Islamic Highness, Abdul's Uncle, has no limits at all. He can go where Her Britannic Majesty can't. Some of the off shore banks' officers found it necessary to be frank and open about the scheme."

"Who knows about this?"

"Your Admiral friend and the Congressman know and wheels are turning," Red said. "Nothing will be public for a while unless there is a leak. This being Washington a leak is always possible. None of the Indian made info went through military intelligence or the CIA. This was special information prepared for certain special persons. The pros want to clear their names."

"All this was done by Indian English majors?"

"Yes, and done for extreme right wing "patriots" who want to turn the county into a theocracy and a cash cow for their own benefit. That is the situation. There are other men in the hunt. The Indian secret service has been trying to track down the source of incorrect information on the subcontinent. The Mexican government is on the trail too. Someone was reporting the Mexican government was going to collapse and flood the United States with refugees. They are pissed. Do you remember Ravi, Abdul's driver? He is the Indian agent working on the scheme."

"Commander Willamette discovered the plot. I'm not sure he understood the full import, but he knew way too much," Red said.

"Who ordered the hit?"

"We don't know. DeBoer probably gave someone the information about the Commander. DeBoer is dead, probably because he could finger the man who ordered the hit," Red said. "I think you know the cast of characters as well as anyone."

"The two most likely suspects are staying at the club now," I said. "I think Hatfield may have brought in new electronic equipment today to set up the blackmail room."

"I can help you with that. He recently purchased miniature German recording cameras and a desk top unit that will broadcast to a remote computer," Red explained.

"Damn, I'll have to move fast!"

"Don't worry too much about that. When he sets the system up, I think they will discover the cameras don't work," Red said. "You are in the cub, we aren't. Do what you can. If you have a problem, we are nearby."

I returned to the club. While I was sweeping the walks, Hadfield, Chance, Edwyn and a man I didn't know went to room 8. They pulled the drapes. I wanted to get in the room, but couldn't figure out any way to do it without drawing attention to me.

Carlton came to the rescue. It was a big night for the club; it had a birthday dinner for one of the older men, Earnest Wright. This was to be black tie, multi-course event with about 40 guests. In addition, they had their regular diners too. The wait and kitchen staff were stretched. "Chance wants a private dinner served in Room 8," Carlton said. "Can you do me a favor and serve it?" I said sure.

"I saw Chance, Hatfield and Edwyn enter with a fourth man, who was he?" I asked.

"That is Robert St. John DeWinter, the chairman of the board of this august institution," Carlton said. "He makes Queen Elizabeth seem like a hippie. He was elected in 2003, but unlike previous chairmen, he rarely visits here."

"He's not the hands on type?"

"To the contrary, he noses into everything, but not in person," Carlton explained." He likes e-mails. I think DeBoer was his spy.

I felt stupid. Mr. DeWinter could be the missing link. The older members complained about the crude and rude newer men. I wondered if they appeared when he became Chairman. The older members were very conservative, but they mostly complained about how awful FDR had been for the nation, and the income tax. Most had inherited wealth and regarded earning a living with distain. DeBoer and Chance weren't like that.

I put on the waiter's uniform and spiffed up my hair. At 7:00, I appeared at the door with a cart of food.

"Where's Troy?" Chance asked.

"He's serving at Mr. Earnest's dinner," I said.

"I'm starved," a man whined. "Let's get some food. I brought the cart in the room. I put a tablecloth on a table and set it up. This was an elaborate dinner, not sandwiches and beer. My mom wasn't fancy, but she did set the table for dinner. Our back door neighbor over the fence was a wealthy banker and his wife, the Robinsons. They were nice people, but fancy. They became good friends. The Robinsons were not good about small domestic emergencies. My parents were. Dad fixed things and when he died, I took care of the little problems.

When I caught a burglar with their silver, Mrs. Robinson gave me a lesson in silverware and the assorted spoons, forks and knives it use to take for a formal dinner. I knew where everything went. Mr. DeWinter and Edwyn approved.

My Mother is a good Presbyterian and firmly believed God moves in mysterious ways and makes his face to shine on the virtuous. Apparently, I was a lot more virtuous than I thought. I was to serve the dinner course by course. Each part of the dinner had to be just right, so it involved multiple trips to the kitchen to get the next course and its associated china.

I didn't stay as they ate, but I did get to hear a portion of the conversation as I removed the previous course and set up the next one. Servants tend to disappear anyway, and I have some skills at looking dumb. Fortunately, DeWinter and Chance were too clever. When I was there, they continued their conversation, assuming I knew nothing. They used coded words only that they would understand.

Chance thought everything was going well. DeWinter and Hatfield were uneasy. "Our problem wasn't just a blip on the radar screen, you know," DeWinter said to Chance.

"Andres, you said our little naval incident was just an accident, but here we are a little more than a month later, and we have a second "little problem." I don't like it."

"We lost all that expensive equipment in the little film studio," DeWinter complained. "That was what my son would call expensive shit. Where in hell is it? It's gone, as is a year's work."

"That company that installed it went bust and the owner vanished," Chance said. He didn't mention the owner hadn't disappeared; he was dead. I had to leave. Fifteen minutes later, I returned with the second course. Each course had its own wine, so I had to open the bottle and submit it for approval. DeWinter gave the approval. He was top dog.

"The whole atmosphere here has changed," Hatfield said, "A couple of congressmen are acting oddly. Senator Thornhill just fell off the radar screen. He's not even returning calls."

"This is Washington. The moon is full and the natives are restless," Chance said.

"Well. If we have a major problem every time there is a full moon, I, for one, will be unhappy," DeWinter said. "I don't want any more "accidents" or "suicides" that can be traced to the Mandrake Club."

I had to leave, but I was back twenty minutes later with desert, and then again for after dinner drinks. The later conversations weren't informative, other than they thought it was important that Carl not know the full extent of the "problems." I assumed the meant the worthy preacher drew the line at murder. There was no question in my mind, all three men knew DeBoer and the Commander's deaths were at the least suspicious, if not murder. That would not have been provable in court. The tone of voice, not the actual words conveyed the meaning.

DeBoer was a close confederate, but his death caused no tears, or even sympathy. I was glad they weren't my business partners. The dinner was over at 9:00. I cleaned up and left them to their conversation. I went to my room. At 10:30, I went to shower and found Jameson and Tony working out. I sense some unease in the air. There were both there hoping for some play time with me, but didn't know they shared a common interest.

I talked with them and let it slip that I knew them both. When we got in the shower, erections cleared up any remaining unease. Jameson took a shine to Tony and sucked him as Tony sucked me. After adjourning to my bedroom, Tony said he was hoping I would fuck him. That was fine with me, but I suggested Jameson fuck him first to open the hole some. Jameson liked that idea, and Tony understood the advantages.

I expected it to be a utility fuck, just a warm up for the main attraction. I didn't expect Tony's ass and Jameson's cock would be a perfect fit. It caught them by surprise too. I deal with disappointment well. I'm not usually a watcher, but this was fun. Jameson's cock looked good, bigger than it had been with me earlier. The prospect of fucking excited him and it. Tony's hole looked miniscule. It seemed impossible Jameson's battering ram would fit. Jameson toyed with the hole, poking and prodding it, but not entering. This drove Tony crazy and soon he was begging Jameson to fuck him.

This technique worked. Tony's hole opened up and relaxed. When Tony was completely relaxed, Jameson made a hard thrust and his cock vanished on the dark side of Tony's sphincter. Tony winced for a second when the knob popped in, and then he relaxed. It was beautiful to see a near perfect merger of cock and ass. Jameson's big knob rubbed Tony's prostate and love tunnel lining, but the thin shaft was no problem for his tight sphincter. They didn't mind me watching, but I'm not sure they noticed. There were in their own world.

Jameson pulled out a few times when he was too close to shooting. Each time he re entered, the hole was more relaxed and welcoming. The undisciplined brain in my cock thought about slipping in the hole on the sly. I decided against that. It was so good for them; I would save my cock for another day. They had a joint orgasm.

I got to bed at 12:30, with my balls still filled with seed and a smile on my face. When I woke the next morning, my brain must have been doing some sorting and figuring as I slept. It was clear Andres was directly associated with the murders. DeWinter and Hatfield were behind the scenes, but both were unhappy about the deaths. They had not authorized the deaths. Anders had acted on his own.

While Andres wasn't the top man, he seemed to have a wide range of action. It was so wide that a measly murder or two demanded only a gentle slap on the wrist. They didn't know about Luther's boss' hit-and-run accident, or anything about the two missing waiters. In my world, killing someone is a big deal. Killing two men is all but unthinkable. It was all in a day's work for Andres. He was delusional psychopath. Edwyn, DeWinter and Hatfield missed that.

It was a rainy day so I put on my leather jacket and hat and went to my favorite Starbucks. The manger I had helped earlier was on duty and I always got a little extra. I sat in the corner reading the Post and drinking my coffee. Red and another man I didn't know came in and joined me. The new man was named David and was dressed informally. I noticed he was wearing an Annapolis ring.

"Have you found out anything?" Red asked. I looked at David uneasily. "It's okay, we're all on the same side," Red said.

I explained my theory about Andres Chance. "I think he ordered the hit, but I don't know who executed it." I whispered.

"You might be interested in knowing Mr. Chance has been in close proximity to several suspicious deaths. His first wife drowned in a boating accident and one of his business partner's was killed in a hit and run accident."

"He is an unlucky man," I said. "Was the wife wealthy?"

"How did you guess?" Red replied. "His wife died in England, and the business partner died in Argentina. Each police department thought it was an isolated occurrence. No one discovered the pattern. By the way, he was alone in the boat when his wife died. If there was foul play, he was the only possible suspect. He said a sudden wind came up and capsized his boat. When he got his wits together, his wife had vanished under the water. Mr. Chance can't swim."

"Apparently he had forgotten how to swim. At Dartmouth he had been on the swim team," David added.

"That clarifies things," I remarked. "Who gets to take him down?"

"Captain Todd, Jameson Todd, is working on filling in the gaps on the fraud elements of the scheme," Red said. "He's not a professional and he was to come to you if things got dangerous. I assume you have met."

"Oh yes," I said. "We have met. I'll keep an eye out on him," I said. I had to get back to work. When I got back, the parking attendant had failed to show up again, so I got to park cars in the rain. Carl Montague arrived at noon. He winked at me. Apparently, he thought our last meeting had been fun. He went to Room 8. It must have been something like a board meeting. I wondered if he knew the other men met the night before without him.

At around three, there was a terrific explosion to the rear of the club. I raced to the back and saw a pillar of smoke and fire rising from what had been Room 8. It was gone. Of course, it was an accident. A small gas line ruptured and exploded. At one time, the Carriage house was the kitchen. The gas line remained long after the club moved the kitchen into the main building. Even a small gas leak can cause a big fire. Carl, Edwyn, Andres and Hatfield were dead. Troy was collateral damage. The police identified the bodies by DNA.

I didn't know who set the hit up. Red could have done it, but it seemed a bit blatant for him. Blowing up a building in a wealthy DC neighborhood could easily bag a senator or congressman. The effort to blackmail Abdul failed, but I'm not sure Abdul's family was the forgiving type. Chance and his associates moved in rough circles, and their scheme was falling apart. Perhaps one of their associates decided to take care of the problem of plea-bargaining.

The cops questioned me for hours. I kept a log of every car that came and went, the time of arrival and departure as well as the license plate number. The Metropolitan Police liked that.

They let us back in the club at 10:00 that evening. Carl Montague's death was big news, but no one knew or cared who the other men were. There was a big funeral for Carl with notables talking about freak accidents. Several days later, I returned to Richmond. The case was closed. I gave a report to Edmund Willamette. He was comforted. Andres Chance had probably murdered his son because the Commander had uncovered a massive fraud scheme.

The scheme never became public; it was too embarrassing to too many people in high places. The government recovered a good deal of the money. They had been stashing the cash in off shore banks who found it necessary to return it to the Treasury. The bankers knew just how accidental the explosion was and weren't taking any chances. There was no way to repair the damage done by the false information provided by the fraudulent companies involved in the scheme.

Afterwards

Several months later, I was in Washington and visited the Mandrake Club. Carlton was the full time director now. Willard's friend Jesus was the gardener. Roosevelt was still the headwaiter and Tony was the new Personal Trainer and lived in my former rooms.

Willard was the new Chairman of the Board. About half the board resigned or retired. I wouldn't say the new board was liberal, but it wasn't a criminal conspiracy any more. Willard instituted a renovation project. This included rebuilding the carriage house and upgrading the facilities in general. That included a new kitchen and greatly improved the exercise area and shower rooms.

Even with the construction in the gardens, they looked great. Pablo was the new horse hung top, but he did a good job keeping it up. Willard had an office in the Club and when I ran into him, he invited me to have dinner at his house that evening. I had no other plans, so I agreed to come.

I got to his farmhouse around 6:00. The gardens looked wonderful. Jesus and his "sons" had done a superb job of clearing out the tangle of vegetation and giving the garden a new lease on life. Willard and Jesus greeted me at the door and we went to his barn. It was mid-winter and it was cold outside.

I was surprised to see Red swimming in the barn's indoor pool. "Clydesdale, I think you know my brother-in-law Redfern?" Willard said. "Make yourself comfortable, several other men will be joining us shortly." By comfortable, he meant naked. That was fine with me. The changing room was to the side. Abdul and Ali emerged from them. Both were pleased to see me if a semi-erect cock is an indicator. Willard had many friends.

Pablo and Carlo were serving drinks. A few minutes later, Carlton, Luther, Roosevelt, Tony and Jameson joined us. Louis, the club's cook, did the cooking with Willard acting as the sous-chef for the night. Conrad, Jack and Johnson were the last guests to arrive. For a second I thought the staff members were there to serve dinner. They were guests and the event had the feel of a neighborhood cook out, if the neighbors were all male, all naked and all gay. The perfect host, Willard distributed tubes of lubricant and bottles of poppers on the appetizer tables.

No one was shy. I knew Willard had a taste for big men. Anyone with a itch up his ass could choose a white, black or brown cock to scratch it. The group was nothing if not open minded and most sampled several.

Jameson came over to me and we caught up of the situation at the Club. He was still there to identify any other members of DeWinter's gang still at large. The Mandrake club had been their clubhouse. The bombing had decapitated the organization, but some spear-carriers was at large, running around like headless chickens. It wasn't an attractive image, but reflected the reality.

Willard was uneasy with the All America Foundation and Andres Chance in particular. When Commander Willamette was murdered, he called Red and told him of his unease. Red was already suspicious of American Intelligence. At first he thought the FBI and CIA had just taken a trip to the wild side. When he found they were as confused by the bad intelligence as he was, Red discovered the All America foundation. The CIA thought the problem was low intelligence and a taste for fantasy in the uppermost levels of the government. They didn't realize a profit-making corporation fed them the bad intel. No one in the government knew the corporation had four full time employees, and some free lancing Indian English majors. Everything was secret and not subject to congressional or departmental oversight. The only qualifications were to be a good American and a good Christian.

Jameson had learned about his prostate and its role as a pleasure-giving organ over the few months since I was last there. Carlton and Tony helped him with that. Jameson wanted me to stretch him wider. Roosevelt was deep in Willard's ass and he was moaning in pleasure. Johnson was on his back with Pedro and Carlo sharing him. Jameson was inspired.

My cock does a good job of filling an ass, with no room left to spare. Jameson was ready. I thought he would be tight and resist. He wanted it bad. He realized it was good when Tony and Carlton fucked him, but instinctively knew a bigger cock would do more. I planned to ease my rod into his ass. Tony lubricated Jameson well and then gave him a deep snort of poppers.

I pushed, and finding no resistance, pushed deeper. A second later, my pubic hair tickled his ass. It was effortless and painless. Jameson's eyes crossed and he almost passed out it was so pleasurable. He needed a big one to reach full sexual satisfaction. I couldn't make a wrong move.

Later that evening he found Roosevelt, Pedro and Carlo's cocks had the same effect. It was a good day for Jameson. The sexual adventures ended when Louis served dinner. As always with Louis, dinner was good.

I sat with Red, Ali and Abdul. They were relaxed. Over the course of the investigation, Ali and Red came to trust each other. When I saw Ali and Abdul together, I realized they were more than just friends. A friend of Ali's was automatically a friend of Abdul. I guess they all were friends with benefits, but they were more than that. They were friends emotionally, intellectually and sexually.

Abdul and Ali were emotionally brothers. Red was the wise father both men needed. Extended Arab families are complex and the sons were often rivals for their father's affection and approval. Red gave that to them along with a great deal of sexual pleasure. The Mandrake Club was Abdul's first brush with danger. They had dealt with it and resolved it. It turned out well.

After dinner, I ended up on my back with Ali's cock in my ass and Abdul's in my mouth. Ali was a crude fucker, but lubricant solved that problem. He calmed down. They kissed as they pumped me from each end. They had simultaneous orgasms. I got a mouthful of prince sperm, as Ali's twitching cock read loaded me. When we broke apart, Ali French kissed me and we shared Abdul's man seed.

Abdul didn't lose his reaction after the orgasm, so he slipped his cock into my sperm filled ass. He liked that enough to shoot a second load in me. As I said, Ali and Abdul were close.

I got up and caught my breath. A short, hairy redneck with Arab cum drooling from his ass might not be everyone's idea of a dreamboat, but in this group, it was a good look. Roosevelt waved at me. I went over to him. "Take a seat," he said. He was on a single chair and was fully erect. "Face away from me. It will fit better. My cock is filling, but not as filling as Roosevelt's member.

As I twitched in his cock, Willard came over and sucked me. I think he really wanted his tongue in my hole with Roosevelt's meat. He wasn't quite able to do that. Fortunately, Abdul and Ali's cum squirted out as the huge organ filled me. It drooled down Roosevelt's bull balls and Willard got his fill.

I thought he was interested in the princely seed, but he took my home brew when the time came. I shot a real gully washer and he took every drop. He also had a hands free orgasm. Naked men can't fake orgasms.

I never found out who set the bomb. Either no one knew, or Red or Ali felt killing four men on foreign soil was too much of a problem. Anders Chance committed three murders and probably five. The waiters never turned up. The bombing solved many problems. I would bet DeWinter and Chance thought the blackmail aspect of the scheme would provide protection for them. It is more likely it sealed their death warrants. "Loose lips sink ships" was the World War II slogan. One loose word could destroy a career.

Perhaps God would welcome Carl Montague to heaven with welcoming arms, but I rather doubt it. I had no doubt Commander Willamette was with the angels, and his father could sleep well.

About the Author

Bob Archman is a retired man living in rural Virginia. He has liked mysteries ever since he got his first Hardy Boy's book in 1957. He also likes Agatha Christie's mature detectives, Hercule Poirot and Jane Marple. He is interested in relationships between mature, hard working men. He tends to write about men who are actively engaged in their jobs and life and happen to be gay, rather than gay men who happen to have a job. A friend of his once asked, "Why be gay and not like sex?" Most of the men in Bob Archman's novels know the answer to that question.

Clydesdale
& COMPANY

A NOVEL BY
Bob Archman

A
BONER
BOOK

Archman

CLYDESDALE & COMPANY

Clydesdale

GOES TO THE HUNT

A NOVEL BY

Bob Archman

Archman

CLYDESDALE GOES TO THE HUNT

Clydesdale
GOES TO A FUNERAL

Archman

CLYDESDALE GOES TO A FUNERAL

A NOVEL BY
Bob Archman

The Cave of the
Blue Bear

Archman

The Cave of the Blue Bear

a novel by
Bob Archman

ARCHMAN

THE BUTLER & THE BARBARIANS

THE BUTLER &
THE BARBARIANS
BY BOB ARCHMAN

A
BOXER
BOOK